Rawhide Robinson Rides a Wormhole

The True Tale of
Bravery and Daring in the Weird West

Books by Rod Miller

Rawhide Robinson *series*
Rawhide Robinson Rides the Range
Rawhide Robinson Rides the Tabby Trail
Rawhide Robinson Rides a Dromedary
Rawhide Robinson Rides a Wormhole

Novels
Cold as the Clay
Father unto Many Sons
Pinebox Collins

Coming Soon!
Silver Screen Cowboy

Rawhide Robinson Rides a Wormhole

The True Tale of
Bravery and Daring in the Weird West

Rod Miller

SPEAKING VOLUMES, LLC
NAPLES, FLORIDA
2022

Rawhide Robinson Rides a Wormhole

ISBN 978-1-64540-695-2

Prologue

Raindrops the size of sage hen eggs raised clouds of dust as they pounded the ground. Rawhide Robinson peeked out from under the dripping brim of his thirteen-gallon hat, wondering at the dusty haze hanging over newly minted mud.

An ordinary cowboy doing ordinary cowboy work, Rawhide Robinson was out hunting cows in the far reaches of grazing land wandered by cattle wearing the "51" brand. "Grazing" overstated the case. Word had it the ranch's name came from the fact that a cow had to walk fifty-one paces between bites of the wilted bunch grass that passed for fodder in this desolate country. Eating at a walk didn't do much when it came to piling on pounds, but somehow the spindly critters survived.

The early afternoon thunderstorm caught the cowboy on the northeast face of the Papoose Range, where he and his horse were beating the brush up and down one draw after another looking for cows and calves, checking their condition and generally keeping track of the far-flung 51 herd. Heavy, black clouds dimmed the sky and distant thunder rumbled, then the storm stampeded over the top of the mountain and lightning sliced the sky, ripping the thunderheads apart and dumping rain on the desert.

Water was rare as pinfeathers on a billiard ball on these ranges, so while the cowboy welcomed the deluge for the grass it might grow, he cursed the discomfort it caused. He loosened the cinches on his saddle, took lead rope in hand and burrowed under the branches of a scrawny cedar tree seeking shelter. The overgrown shrub offered little cover, and Rawhide Robinson was soon soaked from topknot to toenails.

The horse couldn't decide whether to be spooked by the booming thunder and run away, or lay down and roll into a little ball to hide from the spiking lightning. So he stood, spraddle-legged, head hung low, shivering and shaking, eyelids squeezed tight, ears drooping and dripping, rain streaming off his saddle and rump and withers and hocks and brisket and croup and cannons and forearms and fetlocks in sheets, whimpering like a waterlogged dog.

Had the horse's eyes been open when a lightning bolt sizzled the cedar tree, he, like Rawhide Robinson, would have been temporarily turned sightless by the incandescence. But the sodden bovine babysitter was unaware of being briefly blinded as he was rendered utterly senseless by the strike and knocked flat on his back.

Sunshine eventually awakened the recumbent bronc stomper, his eyelids squinting against the bright light. Ever so slowly, Rawhide Robinson coaxed the thin skin of the ocular curtains upward, gave his eyes a thorough knuckle-scrub and sat up to have a look around.

He first noticed the absence of his preferred method of perambulation: the horse was gone. And with it went his reata, canteen, bedroll, grub sack, and saddlebags stuffed with useful bits of this and that. Still somewhat addlebrained from the sudden influx of electricity, the cowboy increased the circumference of his study of the surroundings. There was a vague sense of familiarity in what he saw, but at the same time it all seemed slightly off kilter, although he could not quite put his finger on what was wrong. Seeing no mud or standing water after the remembered deluge, he patted himself from shoulder to chaps to test the dampness of his person.

The cowboy increased again the scope of his vision to scan his environs. The Jumbled Hills and Tikaboo Valley beyond to the east looked as they should, as did the Groom Range to the north. But there was something wrong about the alkali playa below called Groom Lake. Its surface should be as featureless as the top of a sheet-iron stove. Instead, a wide swath as straight as a string cut across the western edge of the dry bed from northwest to southeast, and near its end, almost directly below where the cowboy sat, sat an assemblage of buildings of some kind. Rawhide Robinson studied the layout as best he could in the absence of his collapsible brass telescope (gone, with the other handy gadgets he kept in his saddlebags) but could not make hide nor hair of the place. The buildings looked as if someone had split giant tomato cans from top to bottom and laid them on the ground like tin turtles.

After much effort weighing and measuring every other possibility and finding none to tip the balance, Rawhide Robinson believed the only reasonable choice was to mount shank's mare and hoof it across Groom Lake toward the Tikaboo Valley and headquarters of the 51 Ranch. Unfolding his hinges, the cowboy got himself upright and dusted off the seat of his britches. He stomped his high-heeled boots a time or two to wake up his feet, tugged the brim of his hat down to assure the firmness of its seat, and set off down the slope.

No self-respecting cowboy walks when he can ride, to the point of saddling up for a visit to the outhouse. The unaccustomed means of motion, and the near uselessness of high-topped, high-heeled boots for repeated striding, soon wore blisters on Rawhide Robinson's feet. With every step he cussed the cayuse that abandoned him to his fate and he invented a whole new vocabulary of curse words with which he intended to address the equine absquatulator when next they met.

No sooner had the hobbling cowhand reached the flats than thunder once again filled the sky. Rawhide Robinson stopped. He rotated his head from side to side. He removed his hat to eliminate any possibility of sonic interference. Still, he could not make sense of what he heard. The sky was clear and blue. And, rather than the usual boom and bust of rolling thunder, this outlandish sound grew ever louder to the point of being painful. Clapping his thirteen-gallon hat back atop his head, Rawhide Robinson tugged it down low till it folded his ears, then folded the brim down over them in a hopeless attempt at insulating his hearing gear from the growing roar.

The earth beneath him trembled. The very air oscillated. His body quivered inside and out. He squatted to make himself small. A shadow passed over him. He looked up to see whence it came and a giant flying locomotive, absent its freight train, thundered overhead. The cringing cowboy—stripped of his usual courage in the face of danger—looked on in horror as the giant iron machine dropped ever-closer to a collision with the surface of Groom Lake.

Rawhide Robinson stood. He watched open-mouthed as the machine—whatever it was, as it was now clear it was no train engine—touched down on wheels that appeared out of its belly, rolled along for a time, then pivoted around as smooth as a cutting horse and came back after him. Wanting nothing further to do with the long, skinny, shiny metal pipe with all its sharp points and projectiles and noisy engines, the cowboy shuffled as fast as his tender tootsies would take him across the lakebed in the general direction of the 51 Ranch.

Chapter One

Even through a shroud of sweat and smoke, a mask of dust and grime, the faces of the cowboys glowed in the light of the campfire. It was spring roundup time at the 51 Ranch, and the hands were out with the wagon, gathering cows and calves from the arid range, then exhibiting cowboy and cowhorse skills as they cut calves from the herd, roped hind legs and dragged the bawling bovine babies to the branding fire. There, the ground crew, with motion as precise as the mechanism inside a Swiss watch, burned the "51" brand onto hair and hide, whittled ears with a crop and under-bit on the left and a swallow-fork on the right, and turned pending bulls into steers.

But for today, the work was done, saddles stripped, and supper swallowed. The 51 crew huddled close around the campfire, its warmth fending off the spring evening's brisk desert air. In keeping with the norm on such occasions, the cowboys cradled tin coffee cups in their hands, sipping the soothing brew and absorbing its warmth. Also honoring the tradition of the roundup fire, the relaxing hands shared story and song, poem and proverb. Horse wrecks and cow attacks, fast rides and rope artistry, bronc busting and trail drives and similar subjects near and dear to the hearts of bowlegged beef babysitters everywhere were the order of the day—or evening, as it were.

Standing outside the circle, Matthew Brooks listened in and occasionally offered a comment. As foreman of the 51 Ranch, he oversaw the roundup, making assignments for riding circle and duties at the branding fire. "Beanbelly" Brown rattled around the chuckwagon, cleaning up after the evening meal and getting a head start on breakfast. He cooked at the bunkhouse at headquarters as well as manning the chuckwagon for spring and fall works. The owner of the 51, Dominique Elizondo, checked the progress every few days, kept the chuckwagon supplied, and suggested the next location when it came time to relocate.

Seated in the circle was an ordinary-looking cowboy. Neither short nor tall, not narrow nor wide, this well-traveled cowboy had joined the 51 Ranch crew for the spring roundup. In all things cowboy, he proved himself competent and capable, even, perhaps, a bit above average. He sat without speaking, sipping his coffee, enjoying the yarns as the talk circled the campfire.

"When this roundup is over, I'm tradin' my saddle for a mule harness and takin' up farming," said a mature cowhand called Red (for reasons long since turned white).

"Farming!" a freckle-faced young buckaroo who went by Pinto said. "$%&@#! No self-respecting cowboy would follow a plow!"

"Son," Red said, "when you've spent as many years as I have staring at the south end of northbound cattle, you'll come to realize that lookin' at the backside of a mule has attractions all its own."

"Like what?"

"Oh, I dunno. Sleepin' in a feather bed 'stead of a bedroll propped up by rocks. Or, cuddlin' up to a wife rather than sharin' a bunkhouse with a passel of putrid punchers and packs of pants rats. Eatin' grub that ain't been seasoned with ashes; drinkin' water without havin' to strain out sand and gravel with my teeth."

Matt Brooks said, "Why, Red, you make farming sound downright attractive. Say, any of you boys ever done any farming? Care to compare notes with ol' Red?"

Various voices around the fire offered observations on row-crop agriculture. Some had grown up on farms and had no intention of returning to the life. Others had enjoyed cultivating crops, but primogeniture removed any opportunity to inherit the family farm. The nearest others had been to farm life was eating sourdough biscuits made from flour made from wheat or drinking corn liquor and eating other agricultural comestibles.

Matt said, "How 'bout you, Rawhide? You ever worked a farm?" In asking the question, the cow boss had no idea he had set loose a force of nature.

"Nah. I've been a saddle bum pretty much all my life. But," Rawhide Robinson said before he paused to sip his coffee. "I did help a sodbuster bust some sod one time."

He said no more, allowing the crew to consider the claim.

After a time, Red said, "How did that happen?"

"What do you mean by that?" Pinto said.

Matt said, "Tell us about that."

Other curious cowboys joined the campfire chorus, encouraging Rawhide Robinson to continue his chronicle.

He sipped some more brew and let his audience stew. Then, "Well, boys, it was like this. I was with a crew moving a mixed herd of Texas longhorns up the Goodnight-Loving Trail to stock a ranch up in the Chugwater country in Wyoming. I was riding scout one morning on the Colorado plains when I come across a nester's cabin.

"The house was a soddy, not much bigger than a saddle blanket. A burnt-up wagon, still smoldering, and some busted-up farm implements sat close by. There was a lean-to on one side of the shack for animals, with a low wall of sod around to keep critters penned. I could hear a hog rootin' around in there, and there was a few hens scratching around, but other than that there wasn't no sign of life. Which seemed to me something of a surprise, as the place looked recent."

Again, the cowboy paused for a taste of coffee. He seemed lost in thought or memory and did not continue until encouraged by the impatient prompting of his listeners. "Oh, sorry, boys. Where was I? Right. Anyhow, I reined up there in the yard to have a look-see, when I heard a faint whimper. I rode around to the other side of the soddy and there sat a woman. She was leanin' ag'in the side of the house sobbing softly with tear tracks a-runnin' down her cheeks. Looked downright pitiful, she did. I says, 'Ma'am, are you all right?' and she jumped to her feet quick as a grasshopper. 'Sorry, ma'am,' I says. 'Didn't mean to startle you.'

"She mopped at her face with the tail of her apron and says she didn't hear or see me coming. I asked her what was the matter, and she started up crying all over again. I says, 'You alone here? Where's your man?' After a minute or two she got to where she could talk and told me he was out on the prairie afoot looking to retrieve his mules. Said some rustlers had been by in the night and stole the team and wrecked their implements. Her feller went hunting them.

"She set in to sobbing all over again, said she feared he'd been shot and wouldn't be coming back and she didn't know what she would do and she would likely die out there alone and she was with child and the baby would never see the light of day and if she didn't starve she'd be set upon by marauders and killed and if she lived to see winter she'd freeze to death but didn't think that was likely as she would swell up and die from snakebite long before the weather turned or get struck by lightning or sucked up by a tornado or run over by a buffalo stampede or the well would run dry and she'd die of thirst and so on and so on and so on.

"I ain't never seen such misery in a person, particularly one that young—woman didn't look no more than maybe eighteen years old, if that. Anyway, by that time I seen someone coming and she said it was her husband and she ran to meet him and darn near upended him with all her hugging and squeezing."

Rawhide Robinson dumped the dregs from his tin mug and moseyed over to the cook fire to refill it from the pot. In the traditional "man at the pot" ritual, he offered to top off any cup needing it done. Instead, his audience harangued him to get back to the story.

"Now, boys, take it easy. As Jean-Jacques Rousseau philosophized, 'Patience is bitter, but its fruit is sweet.' "

Pinto said, "John Jock who?"

"Rousseau," Rawhide Robinson said. "Lived in Switzerland a long time ago. Along about the middle of the 1700s, if I recollect correctly."

"What's he got to do with anything?"

Red erupted. "He ain't got nothin' to do with it, Pinto! Now hush up and let the man tell his story. Rawhide, my patience is wearin' thin, Rousseau or no Rousseau. Get on with it!"

Rawhide Robinson smiled and sipped his coffee. "Well, I noticed this sodbuster hadn't busted any sod. I asked him about it, and he said he had only just finished the house and such and was getting ready to start plowing when them night riders showed up and stole his team of mules and wrecked his plow. It was late in the season, and he feared he'd lose his homestead on account of not being able to put in a crop and prove up.

"Well, them nesters looked so pitiful I couldn't see abandoning them to their fate. So I told them stay put and I would think of something. I rode back to the herd pondering and ruminating and contemplating and considering and cogitating all the way, and by the time the drive made it near to where them homesteaders was, I figured I had an idea."

Again, Rawhide Robinson paused in the telling to lubricate his talking apparatus with hot coffee. And, again, his listeners ranted and raved for him to carry on. And—after a suitable interval as anticipation built—he did.

"What I did, boys, was cut out a big old cow—you know the kind I mean, whose horns was long and sharp and curled—and a docile old bull and drove them over to where that boy wanted to break ground."

"Oh!" Red said. "I see! You turned them critters into oxen and yoked them up and hitched them to the plow."

Rawhide Robinson smiled. "No, Red. I thought of that, naturally, but that boy had no yoke for an ox team, and as you recall, the plow was busted anyway."

"So what did you do?"

"Well, I'd brung a stout length of rope from the hoodlum wagon, and I tied a honda and built a loop in both ends—"

"—Both ends!?"

"Both ends. Then I lassoed the big old horns of that cow, tripped her up, rolled her on her back, and hog-tied all four legs, hock and dewclaw. Then, I roped that bull with the other end of that fat lariat so, you see, that belly-up cow was latched onto that bull. Got the picture?"

It took a few questions, a few answers, and some wagging and waving of hands and arms, but soon enough everyone at the campfire could visualize what Rawhide Robinson had wrought that day on the Colorado plains. But their imaginations ended there.

"Then what?" they asked as one.

"Oh, fellers! It's as plain as the noses on your ugly mugs! What I done was herd that brawny old bull back and forth across where that nester had staked out his fields. Of course, that bull dragged that belly-up cow behind him, and that cow's long ol' horns sliced into that sod and turned it over slicker than a two-bottom moldboard plow. I had them fields plowed and me and the cattle back to the herd in time for supper."

The taken-aback cowhands labeled Rawhide Robinson's babble as so much baloney, balderdash, bunk, and, as one would expect, bull#*$@.

But, of course, Rawhide Robinson stood by the story, swearing to its veracity with a smile on his face and a twinkle in his eye.

Chapter Two

The freckle-faced 51 Ranch cowboy called Pinto, being young and full of vinegar, aspired to be the outfit's rough-string rider.

With spring roundup and branding in the books, it was time, on the 51, as it was on many a ranch, to run in the remuda, the cavvy, the saddle band, the horse herd, and cut out the young, unbroken broncs and start them down the trail that would lead to their becoming usable working cowhorses.

Pinto could hardly wait.

But he would have to wait, for when the cowboys hazed the first unbroken horse into the round corral, foreman Matt Brooks said, "Say, Rawhide—you've been around some. You spent any time takin' the rough off broncs?"

Rawhide Robinson smiled. "Oh, I've forked a few in my time. Truth is, though, I can barely stay aboard a buckboard, let alone a horse that's got any buck in him."

The foreman smiled. Cowboys, particularly the best of them, were often dismissive of their abilities and, given Rawhide Robinson's performance during spring works, Matt sensed that was the case with his newest hand. "Well," he said, drawing out his orders and pointing out a particular critter. "Why not see if you can lace your kack on that horse there and see what happens."

As Rawhide Robinson threw his saddle over the top rail, untied his lass rope and shook out a loop, the rest of the 51 Ranch cowboys climbed up the fence to take a seat in the spectator section. Pinto whined and whimpered and murmured and moaned at being relegated to the gallery, but Matt told him to hold his water and take a seat, as he might learn something—a prospect at which the young cowboy snorted.

With an effortless hoolihan loop, Rawhide Robinson had a rope around the bronc's neck in an instant. He reeled in his slack and planted his heels in the dust. The horse fought the rope, as such horses in such circumstances are wont to do, and the cowboy's footwear plowed a pair of parallel furrows in the dirt. Someone opened the gate, and Rawhide Robinson hazed the horse into the round pen. Working his way to the snubbing post in the middle of the corral, he walked around it to secure the rope and slowly but surely reeled in the horse as it continued testing the strength of the rope.

After a time, the horse settled down some. And when he did, the cowboy fetched a hackamore and slipped the headstall over the quivering bronc's ears and the bosal over his nose. Slipping the lariat off the horse's neck, he tied the *mecate*—a hair rope that did double duty as a lead rope and reins—around the post.

Pinto, from his perch on the top rail, derided Rawhide Robinson for his cautious approach, laughing all the while and tossing barbs. From time to time Matt, or Red, or one of the other cowboys would tell him to hush up, but it was no cure—another round of ridicule soon erupted.

But Rawhide Robinson ignored the young cowboy, concentrating, instead, on the horse. He fetched a saddle blanket and allowed the skittish horse to smell it. He slowly swung the blanket beside the horse, letting it brush and touch him, rubbed it against his legs, circling around and letting the blanket do its work from every angle. For his part, the horse snorted and pawed, shying away from the touch and hanging back on his tether. Within minutes, the fear—if not gone—was mitigated and the horse merely trembled and occasionally flinched at the blanket. The cowboy slung the blanket over the horse's back and let it sit, removed it and repeated the process several times.

He let it sit, then set the saddle atop it. Again, the horse hung back, tossed his head, and shied away, but Rawhide Robinson followed. In time, he reached the cinch, threaded the latigo, and secured the saddle. Then, the cowboy squatted on his spurs in the scant shade of the fence and mopped his sweaty forehead and face with his bandana.

"What's the matter, Rawhide?" Pinto said. "You a-scared to get on 'im?"

"Nah. Just letting him soak for a minute whilst I catch my breath."

The youngster laughed. "I say you're afraid."

The cowboy knotted the wild rag back around his neck. "Well, son, I notice you've got a whole lot to say."

Red threw his hat into the ring with, "That's right, kid—you got a lot to say, but I ain't seen you do much."

Pinto's complexion reddened beneath the freckles and he quivered like the bronc. "Get that ol' geezer out of the corral and I'll show you what I can do."

"Calm down, Pinto," Matt said. "You'll get a chance to get piled soon enough."

"See if I do!"

Red laughed. "We'll see, all right, kid. We'll see."

Rawhide Robinson stood, screwed his thirteen-gallon hat down tight, adjusted the belt on his leggings and approached the horse. The bronc eyed him warily. The cowboy untied the mecate from the snubbing post, slung the end around the horse's neck and tied it to the bosal, creating a continuous rein. Scratching the bronc's nose and rubbing its neck, he led it around a tight circle, then again. The cowboy grabbed the cheek piece on the hackamore and pulled the horse's head around, reached his foot to the stirrup and stood, swinging his leg over the saddle and finding the other stirrup. He released the hackamore and wiggled his way into a deep seat.

The horse's ears twitched, flickering forward and back, then laid back flat as he gathered his muscles and leapt out of his tracks. Rawhide Robinson kept the rein taut as the horse crow-hopped across the pen, turned away from the fence and bucked the other way. Before he reached the opposite fence, the cowboy put pressure on the left side of the rein, forcing the horse into a circle. Soon, the animal stopped trying to buck and trotted around the pen. Touching his spurs to the bronc's belly, Rawhide Robinson urged him into a slow lope, turning him one way then the other in figure-eights and circles, teaching the horse to respond to the rein.

He walked the horse. Trotted. Loped. Backed up. Turned circles. Started. Stopped. The horse worked up a good sweat, and so did the cowboy. He reined up the horse next to the fence, stepped out of the saddle and loosened the cinch, then pulled his kack and propped it on the top rail. "Matt, I wouldn't call him broke, of course, but a few more saddles and he'll be fit to ride circle on. My guess is he'll make a good cow pony. He's light on his feet, so he might even make a cutting horse."

Matt told one of the cowboys to open the gate, and Rawhide Robinson led the horse through, patted his neck, stripped the hackamore, and shooed the horse toward the others huddled in the corner of the larger corral. Matt walked to the bunch and peeled off a roan gelding and shooed it into the round pen.

"All right, Pinto. This one's yours," he said.

"Show us how it's done," Red said with a laugh.

Pinto scowled as he carried his saddle into the pen and dropped it in the dirt. He pulled his rope, built a loop, and took a shot at the horse as it trotted around the round pen. Just as the loop dropped to settle around the bronc's neck, it ducked its head and the lariat caught nothing but dust. He cast another loop with the same result. On the third try, the loop found its mark. Pinto pulled it tight, wrapped the tail of the rope around his backside and leaned back onto it, starting a tug-of-war. The horse faced the young cowboy, shaking its head, backing away, rearing up, and dragging Pinto along. The horse tired, and the dragging stopped.

"Slim!" he hollered to his friend on the fence. "Ear 'im down!"

Slim slid off the fence and followed the rope to the horse. As the frightened animal thrashed and tossed its head, Slim jumped up and wrapped the horse's head in his arms and hung on. As the tossing continued, he found an ear with one hand and gave it a hard twist, which halted the thrashing. Slim pulled the head lower and sunk his teeth into the ear.

Thus distracted, the bronc stood more or less still as Pinto cinched down his saddle. The horse pitched another fit when Slim turned loose its ear while Pinto slid on a hackamore, then Slim clamped his jaws on the cartilage again as Pinto climbed aboard.

"Let's dance!" he said, once in the saddle.

Slim spit out the ear and jumped clear. The horse stood for a few seconds, as if regaining awareness of its whereabouts. Then, with a bawl and a beller, it shot into the air and lit stiff-legged like a pile driver. Pinto felt the effect of it in every joint of his spine. The bronc lunged, loosening the rider's seat in the saddle, stuck its head between its legs, and kicked hind legs high. That move loosened Pinto altogether, and he launched forward as if shot from a cannon, clearing the horse's head and landing on his own.

But this was not Pinto's first rodeo, and he knew to go limp and roll with the impact. While his body made the landing without injury, his pride and temperament did not.

He scrambled to his feet and watched the horse buck and kick around the pen. Slim stepped in front of the horse and it reversed direction, only to find Pinto there.

The disgruntled cowboy managed to grab hold of a trailing rein and jerked the horse around. He yanked and tugged and pulled, jerking the horse one way then the other. The horse reared and backed away, then Pinto went to work with the quirt strapped to his wrist.

He landed only a few sharp blows to the horse's head before he found himself, once again, eating dirt.

Pinto again scrambled to his feet. Before gaining his balance, he found himself lifted off the ground and nose to nose to Rawhide Robinson.

"Put me down, old man!" the boy said.

Rawhide Robinson shook Pinto like a dog does a dead jackrabbit, then threw him to the ground. The youngster crabbed away on his backside as the older cowboy pursued, wagging a finger in the boy's face to emphasize his every word.

"No cowboy treats a horse like that! That bronc tossed you fair and square. If you was any kind of the hand you think you are, you would have dusted off your britches and climbed back on to try him again. Abusin' an animal thataway won't make a cowhorse, only an outlaw."

Rawhide Robinson reached down and grabbed the retreating cowboy's shirtfront and hauled him to his feet. Again nose to nose, he unleashed another tirade.

"Boy, I don't care if you ever amount to a cowboy or not. But I'll tell you this—if you've got a notion to be a bronc buster, a bronc breaker, a bronc squeezer, a bronc twister, a bronc peeler, a bronc snapper, a bronc scratcher, a bronc stomper, a bronc fighter, or any other kind of a hand at breaking horses, you'd best learn to treat broncs with respect. Otherwise, if one of them bangtails don't bust you to pieces, some cowboy—one worthy of the name—will!"

With that, Rawhide Robinson shoved the red-faced, freckle-faced young cowboy back down to the ground, turned on the high heels of his high-top Texas boots and stomped off toward the bunkhouse, cussing himself every step of the way for losing his temper.

Chapter Three

Pinto spent the next few weeks walking on eggs after getting dressed down in the round corral by Rawhide Robinson. But the boy's enthusiasm for topping off broncs did not diminish. Red, an experienced hand who no longer forked snuffy horses owing to his age, took the kid under his wing and helped him learn the finer points of turning unbroken horses into working cowhorses. Pinto even turned to Rawhide Robinson for advice from time to time, and the customarily congenial cowboy complied, contributing to the kid's capabilities.

The long days of summer at the 51 Ranch kept the hands horseback and hunting cattle, making sure the herd did not wander too far, and pushing them back toward headquarters when they did. Mostly, the cows and calves congregated near the scarce watering holes. There were few distractions for the cowboys—an occasional Saturday night trip to Alamo. The small town offered few diversions, save, perhaps, a dance with the Mormon girls at a church social, or a drink at the quiet saloon.

Most of the cowboys were content, most of the time. But, on occasion, boredom would boil over and someone would haul his freight some eighty miles northeast to the town of Pioche. Amenities in the mining boomtown were manifold, but with the pleasure came danger. Tinhorn gamblers ran rampant, fleecing miners of their pay. Gunfights were commonplace and kept gravediggers busy. Word had it that more than seventy victims of violence were planted in the cemetery before burial of a body dead from natural causes.

Rawhide Robinson, having seen his fill of tough towns in his trail driving days, saw no need to partake of the pleasures of Pioche.

Mines enriched Pioche, and the quest for minerals saw many a boomtown come, and almost as many go, in the Silver State. Round Mountain. Manhattan. Tonopah. Gold Field. Gold Point. Bonnie Claire. Rhyolite. Delamar. The bones of these and other glory holes were scattered across the deserts, as were still-productive mines. Given Nevada's mineral wealth, at times it seemed there were as many prospectors wandering the 51 range as there were cattle.

One evening, toward the end of the sun's long slide to its resting place beyond the mountains, as the 51 cowboys sat in the shade of the bunkhouse digesting bellyfuls of beef, beans, and biscuits, a prospector wandered into the yard. The burro he led bristled with pick and shovel handles; pots and pans clinked and clanged in time with his dainty hoofbeats.

Stopping a short stone's throw from the relaxed assemblage of cowboys, the sourdough said, "You-uns mind if I water Ol' Nightingale?"

"Nightingale?" more than one of the cowboys said with a laugh.

"Yep. That's what I call her. Desert Canary—Arizona Nightingale—folks call burros all manner of such melodious names, so I thought I'd borrow it outright. Fact is, this is the eighth time I've hung that particular moniker on a donkey of mine." He paused to spit a stringy stream of tobacco juice into the dust, the tail end of which clung to his beard. The stripes of brown stains in the white and gray fleece testified it was not the first time. "If you're lucky, and kindly allow us to bed down here for the night, Ol' Nightingale might see fit to serenade you-uns in the moonlight."

Permission was granted and hospitality extended, going so far as to dish up what beef and beans and biscuits remained on the stove in the bunkhouse kitchen for the prospector, and pouring a bait of oats for Ol' Nightingale.

"Gold Pan Gibson is what most folks call me," the sourdough told the ranch riders as he shoveled in his supper. "Been scratchin' around these hills for nigh on ten years now. 'Fore that, I prospected up on Davis Mountain near the Washoe country. Been in the Black Hills, the Oquirrhs, Superstitions, Rockies, Sierras, and Dragoons. Prospected Grasshopper Creek, Cripple Creek, Douglas Creek, Furnace Creek, Potato Creek, and Willow Creek. Death Valley, Pleasant Valley, Honey Valley, Moreno Valley, Lake Valley, Holcomb Valley—well, you-all get the idea. Been prospectin' longer'n most of you-uns has been breathin' air."

The cowboys peppered the prospector with questions, and he supplied answers by the barrel full—as if this conversation were his first in quite some time, which it probably was. They learned he had discovered several rich claims, but sold them off for little more than a grubstake. "Prospectin' is like a disease with me, you see. Can't leave it be. But I got no interest whatsoever in mining."

The prospector regaled the cowboys with stories and did not wind down until well into the night. A question was floated as to whether anyone else among them knew anything of mining. No one did.

Except Rawhide Robinson.

He told a tale of placer mining on the Colorado River in Arizona Territory with an old sourdough much like Gold Pan Gibson that left his audience aghast. "I did not much enjoy my foray into mineral extraction," he said. "All that digging was too much like work for a cowboy like me. My hands just ain't fit to a shovel handle."

A brief intermission allowed the prospector to whittle a fresh chew off his plug, others to roll smokes, and one and all to freshen up the brew in their coffee mugs.

"I did see a deal one time that made me think mining might not be so bad after all," Rawhide Robinson said when all were settled in. Then he seemed to drift away as he nursed his coffee.

"Well, what about it?" Slim said.

Red said, "Rawhide? You gonna tell us?"

"C'mon! Talk!" said another cowboy.

Gold Pan Gibson said, "I'd be mighty interested in hearing about it myself."

Waking out of his reverie, Rawhide Robinson said, "It was in Utah, where the Tintic mines are. No placer mining in that country. It's all underground, and from what them miners around there told me, there weren't no such thing as easy digging."

"What were you doing in Utah, anyways?" Pinto said.

"Well, it's like this. The army has a fort up there near Salt Lake City. Fort Douglas, as I recollect. I was helping to bring in a string of remounts for the cavalry—they had a troop of Buffalo Soldiers assigned there, and that herd of horses was for them. After we delivered the horses, I thought to wander a little and, for no particular reason, found myself riding across the Goshen Valley toward the Tintic Mountains.

"I come across this big ol' freight wagon bogged down in a swampy little creek. Being naturally inclined to helpfulness—as you-all are aware—I helped the teamster haul that wagon out of the mire. I got a mite curious about what he was hauling, as I could hear something scritching and scratching around in there, along with some yips and barks and chirps. Couldn't see in, on account of the high sides and tarp over the top. So I asked that feller what he was packing. 'Prairie dogs,' he said."

The revelation resulted in choruses of disbelief, dubiety, and incredulity among the cowboys.

Rawhide Robinson raised a hand to stem the tide and said, "Now, boys, calm yourselves. I know it sounds nonsensical, but that's what he said. Fact is, I was skeptical myself, so I decided to tag along just to see for myself what he was up to. He weren't too happy about that, but since I'd helped him get his wagon unstuck he allowed as how I could go along if I promised not to spread it around what he was up to."

Again, the raconteur took a recess, sipping his coffee, scratching his chin, and resetting his thirteen-gallon hat.

"Well!?" an impatient cowboy yelled, accompanied by mumbling and murmurs of the impatient sort from the others. "What was he up to?"

"I'll get to it boys—take it easy." After another sip of coffee, he continued. "Mining was just taking hold on the Tintic Mountains at the time, and this feller, he figured to get in on the ground floor. But, as Gold Pan Gibson here will attest, locating a likely claim ain't easy. And it takes time. What with all the prospectors thereabouts, he didn't figure time was on his side. That's where the prairie dogs come in."

The cowboys, by this time, were on the edges of their seats, so to speak. Rawhide Robinson tested their patience before continuing.

"Rather than poke around with his pick and shovel, what he did was turn loose a pack of prairie dogs and let them do the digging. As they burrowed into the mountainside, he'd nose around in the dirt and rocks they pitched out of the holes for any sign of color. If nothing looked promising, why, he'd pack up his prairie dogs and relocate. He covered that country right quick, he did. Had the rest of them prospectors right envious at his inventiveness, he did."

The cowboys cogitated for a time on what the cowboy chronicler said. Some expressed wonder. Others doubt. Some disagreed such a thing could happen. Others allowed it could. Rawhide Robinson swore it did.

"I seen it, boys, with my own eyes. I was there. It's as genuine as the freckles on Pinto's face."

Gold Pan Gibson said, "But did it work? Did he find anything?"

"Oh, sure." Rawhide Robinson said. "Staked a whole passel of claims. Read later in the newspaper a bunch of them claims turned into rich mines—Black Jack, Dragon, Mammoth, Armstrong, Tintic Standard, Chief, Uncle Sam, Mayday, Northern Spy, Iron Blossom…there were others, but I don't recollect the names of any more of them."

The cowboys continued to ponder. Gold Pan Gibson, on the other hand, set into packing his possibles and loading them aboard Ol' Nightingale in a fury.

"What is it you're doing, Gold Pan?" Rawhide Robinson said. "I thought you were spending the night."

"Not me," the prospector said. "No time. I got to go get me some prairie dogs."

Chapter Four

Every morning, Matt Brooks stood, coffee mug in hand, in the yard in front of the bunkhouse door. The hands filtered out in the gray dawn and formed a semicircle around the straw boss, also enjoying their last taste of coffee before going to work. Most mornings, most men were sent out horseback—often on a green horse fresh from the breaking pen to further its training—to some far point on the 51 range to circle back on a parallel path. Along the way, the cowboys were to tally the cows and calves, note the locations of the range bulls, and doctor any cow critters that required attention. In a word, the men were to prove the contention that "cowboy" is a verb as much a noun.

That morning, Rawhide Robinson's assignment was to ride at a long trot across the Tikaboo Valley—where the whereabouts of stock was nearby and well known—through the Jumbled Hills to the Emigrant Valley, and make camp in the Papoose Range after scouring as much of the east slope of the mountain as daylight allowed. Come the next morning, the cowboy was to hunt cows along the rest of the draws and ravines and canyons along the range, then ride back to headquarters across the dry playa of Groom Lake. Barring unforeseen difficulties, he should complete the ride home in the dark and spend a short night in his bunkhouse bed.

Stuffing a greasy sack with grub for the trip and tying his bedroll behind the cantle of his saddle, Rawhide Robinson put the soon-to-rise sun at his back and rode out of 51 Ranch headquarters to once again accomplish the kind of ordinary cowboy work to which he had devoted his life.

Little of note happened that day. Among one bunch of cows shaded up in a shallow draw in the Papoose he espied a 51 cow missed in the spring gather—an obvious assumption, given that the heifer calf at her side wore long ears and a slick hide. Urging the horse to work, he slowly cut the cow and calf from the bunch, then separated the calf from its mother, and tossed a soft loop over the calf's head and tied it off to the saddle horn. Trusting the young horse to hold the rope taut as the calf struggled, he dismounted, hooked an elbow around the rope and followed it to the calf. He hoisted one of its front legs, grabbed a handful of skin at the flank, and tipped the bellowing calf over as its mama snuffled and moaned and contemplated an attack.

With the calf hog-tied, Rawhide Robinson scraped out a hole with the sole of his boot and kindled a branding fire. Lacking a running iron—which could get a cowboy a short ride to the end of a hanging rope on the open range—he tossed an old cinch ring from his saddlebags into the flames. As it heated, he cut the 51 Ranch's registered earmarks on the calf's ears. It continued to beller and the mother continued to pace.

But it wasn't until the cowboy laid the red-hot cinch ring, grasped between crossed sticks, to the calf's hide that the baby's protests prompted action on its mama's part. Rawhide Robinson had no sooner finished burning the long stroke of the "1" to complete the "51" on the calf's ribs when he felt the cow's hot breath then the jolt of her forehead between his shoulder blades. He tumbled across the tethered calf and kept rolling, rising to his feet, hat in hand, as the mad cow scurried around her baby and lined up for another shot at the offending cowboy.

It took several blows from his thirteen-gallon hat—along with a stream of salty language not fit to appear in print—as Rawhide Robinson backpedaled and swatted the cow in the face to finally discourage her. But when she'd had enough of the unaccustomed treatment, she trotted away and turned to face the cowboy, considering another defensive foray to protect her young. Taking advantage of the lull in the action, Rawhide Robinson untied his pigging string, grabbed the calf by the tail and boosted it to its feet.

The next job at hand was a frantic attack on the flaming brush ignited by the wayward cinch rig-cum-branding iron. With the flames stomped out, the smoldering grass trampled to ash, and any sign of heat or smoke extinguished, Rawhide Robinson decided the small branding fire may as well be replenished and put into service as a campfire. The sun was already well behind the Papoose Range, and this spot, albeit a dry camp, would do the job as well as another.

Morning dawned clear and warm, and Rawhide Robinson watched the shadows retreat across the valley as the sun climbed. He packed up his rough camp, rolled and tied up his bed, and continued his work. As the air heated with the ascending sun, clouds blossomed in the southwest and grew taller and darker as they drifted overhead. By afternoon, the sky was thick and heavy and distant thunder rolled across the sky. Rain fell, first a drizzle, then a sprinkle. Lightning flashed, and the thunder that earlier rumbled now crashed, and the rain poured down in drops of a size that could stun a steer. When the soil became mud and turned slippery, testing the young horse's footing, and lightning bolts rained down with the rain, Rawhide Robinson decided it was time to take shelter.

The desert scrub on the hillsides offered little in the way of shelter. A scrawny cedar tree appeared through the deluge, and the cowboy decided its scant cover might be the best available. Another nearby lightning strike and the instant thunder that near knocked him from the saddle sealed the deal. He dismounted and crawled under the fragrant shrub's limbs and branches, lead rope in hand to secure the nervous horse.

As the downpour kept pouring down, a soggy, squatting Rawhide Robinson shivered while his sodden, spraddle-legged steed quivered. An explosion of brilliant light and concussion of booming thunder did not have time to register in the cowboy's brain before knocking him flat in the mud and water, all awareness gone in a flash.

Chapter Five

Rawhide Robinson would never know if the storm passed and the clouds cleared and the glare of the sun awakened him later that same afternoon. Or, whether the day had passed, and the night, and the morning, and the sun assaulting his eyelids belonged to the next day. Or for that matter, the day after that or another day altogether.

The awakening was a slow one, with the discombobulated cowboy regaining his faculties in fits and starts. Among the first facts to wend its way into his consciousness was the absence of a horse. Rawhide Robinson cussed the cayuse under his breath, but was not surprised his mount had skedaddled. Self-preservation is bred in the bones of prey animals, whether fleeing from a cougar with a meal on his mind, or a violent cloudburst with its frightening sturm and drang.

He sat up stiffly, wondering at the ache in his bones and pain in his muscles and stiffness in his joints. Somehow, he did not feel himself. But he did feel damp. His chaps were heavy and spongy, his shirt clammy and clingy, his feet felt humid inside his boots. The rest of the world—at least the parts of it visible from where he sat—did not appear to share the moisture. He scuffed the spur on the heel of his boot back and forth, stirring up a haze of dust from the dry dirt. The hillside on which he sat appeared parched. That it would be so following such a storm surprised—no, confused—him. The valley below appeared likewise dry. A dust devil crept skyward across the white expanse of the alkali flat called Groom Lake.

And then he saw it.

A trail, a path, a wide road stretched across the lakebed where nothing but more of the empty playa had been before. Huddled at the edge of the dry lake was a complex of strange structures. Glints of sunlight off their surface suggested the buildings were made of metal. Their odd shape was unlike any building Rawhide Robinson had ever seen. Nothing described them as well as their looking like giant tomato cans sheared down the middle and lying on their sides, nestled in the dirt like discarded tins in the desert. Except there was nothing random in their arrangement—everything was precisely aligned and systematically arranged—the buildings, the roads between and around them, the yards, and the empty lots tucked between.

It looked to the cowboy like a curious city of sorts. Except there was no sign of life. All was quiet. If there were people associated with the tin can community, they were all inside.

Perplexed, perturbed, and puzzled, Rawhide Robinson started down the hill. There was no alternative to walking, and no place to go but back to the 51 Ranch headquarters. As he slid and stepped and shuffled and stumbled and slipped and skidded downslope, he wondered at the absence of any sign of livestock. No cow chips, no pasture flapjacks, no meadow muffins, no road apples were in evidence. Occasionally he saw pellets planted by mule deer, and scat from other creatures, but no sign of cattle, horses, mules, sheep, or any other domesticated animal.

Something was wrong with the world, and the confused cowboy could not fathom what, exactly, it was. So he kept walking, even as his boots—built for riding—wore blisters on feet as unaccustomed to walking as the boots. As he made his way onto the playa, alkali dust drifted up from the disturbance and coated his boots and the bottoms of his leather leggings, even sifting beneath the chaps to soil the hem of his trousers. As he limped sore-footed across the lakebed, Rawhide Robinson kept an eye on the complex of buildings, but they sat silent and still as if abandoned.

Memories of the thunderstorm returned with a faint and distant roar. The cowboy scanned the sky, but saw nary a cloud. The sound grew quickly, rumbling air and earth alike. So explosive, so powerful, was the ever-intensifying roar that he wondered if it originated with an unseen freight train. But even that noise could not compare with what now pained his ears. He squatted and pulled the brim of his thirteen-gallon hat over his ears. The rowels on his spurs turned, the jinglebobs sung. Vibrations encompassed the cowboy and the earth beneath his feet. He ducked even deeper when a huge shadow covered him.

So close it seemed he could touch it, a giant silver cylinder roared overhead. Other cylinders attached to the sides, as well as the large tube itself, had sharpened ends, and what looked like stubby furled wings stretched from the sides. He felt the heat and smelled the smoke that streamed behind the flying locomotive—for he had no other machine with which to compare it.

Rawhide Robinson watched in horror as the contraption dropped ever closer to the ground. Soon, he believed, it would plow into the lakebed. Instead, wheels dropped out of its belly and it settled onto the long, straight road on the lakebed.

Although the roar was still loud, the terrorized ranahan popped off his hat like a cork from a bottle and reset it in a more comfortable position. He still quivered and shivered from the close encounter with death, chalking it up to luck that the machine had missed him in its attempt to mow him down.

His stomach filled his throat when he saw it pivot around and aim itself in his direction. The roar of whatever power propelled it surged as it readied for another attempt on his life. He looked around in near panic for shelter, but saw only the naked expanse of the dry bed of Groom Lake.

Rawhide Robinson would not simply stand still and await death. When the time came, he would use any means necessary to resist the threat the machine offered. But until that time, he would make time toward the 51 Ranch as fast as a lame but spirited shank's mare could carry him.

Chapter Six

Risking a backward glance from time to time, Rawhide Robinson realized the thing was not after him after all. Instead, it rolled into one of the buildings and disappeared behind giant sliding doors. Despite the curiosity that often overwhelmed him, he wanted nothing more to do with whatever that thing was that swooped down on him like a bald eagle after a fish. Another day, maybe, but not this time.

Just when he had grown accustomed again to the quiet of the high desert as he plodded along, another sound invaded the cowboy's ears. He turned and watched what looked for all the world like four stubby buckboards wheeling his way. Doffing his hat, he scratched his head at the fact that no horses or mules or oxen or other means of motivation pulled the wagons. They appeared to move on their own, like a railroad engine, but with no rails beneath them. All were painted a shade of green reminiscent of day-old droppings from cows on good grass, and the men—four in each carriage—wore clothing of the same hue, topped off by blue hats that looked like the sliced-off end of an eggshell.

The buggies roared up beside him, two to either side, wheeled around to circle and face him and skidded to a stop as the men bailed out, surrounding the flummoxed ranch hand with pointed rifles. One uniformed man, slower to climb down than the others, approached the confounded cowboy. He stood inches away and leaned into Rawhide Robinson, stopping when their noses nearly touched.

"What the hell do you think you're doing?"

Ire raised, Rawhide Robinson hollered back with equal vehemence. "Who's askin'?"

The man took a step back. "I'll ask the questions, you trespassing saddle tramp! What are you, some kind of protester?"

The cowboy only glowered.

"Well!? Who are you? Why are you here? What do you want? Who sent you?"

Rawhide Robinson touched the brim of his thirteen-gallon hat with a forefinger and slid the lid back on his head. The motion prompted metallic clicks and clacks and slides and snaps as the encircling soldiers readied their weapons to fire. He turned in a circle, eyeing his captors with curiosity.

"I take it you-all are soldiers," he finally said. "Can't say I recognize the uniforms. And you must be the man in charge," he said with a nod toward the man with stripes on his sleeves. "You some kind of officer or something?"

"First off, we're not soldiers. We're airmen. United States Air Force Security Police. Second, I am a Sergeant, not an officer. Third, hows about you answer my questions—"

"—How about you-all point them rifles somewhere else. I ain't inclined to palaver with a gun to my head. You want to talk to me, then you-all best show some manners, Sergeant."

At some unseen signal, three of the men behind the cowboy closed in, one grabbed his collar, the others an upper arm each, and forced him face down into the dust. They wrenched his arms behind his back and he heard the ratcheting teeth of the handcuffs as they gripped his wrists—tighter than necessary, he thought.

The airmen loaded Rawhide Robinson into the back seat of one of the buggies and away they went across the dry surface of Groom Lake. The speed discombobulated the cowboy and he ducked his head as low as it would go to keep the wind from blowing his thirteen-gallon hat off his head. The soldiers on either side, pressed tight owing to the narrow seat, laughed.

"Don't worry 'bout losing that hat, cowboy. You ain't likely to be needing it much longer."

"Oh? Why's that?" Rawhide Robinson muffled from below.

"On account of where you're going they'll probably cut your head off."

The folded-up cowboy swallowed hard and thought it best to stay silent. Soon enough, the roaring box he rode in shuddered to a stop and the rumble of the engine died with a cough. The airmen stepped out of the conveyance and the one on the left grabbed Rawhide Robinson's arm and jerked him over the side and stood him on the ground.

"You're a big, strong sort of feller, ain't you."

The airman did not speak. With a nod of his head, he showed the cowboy which way to go. They followed the sergeant through a door cut in the end of one of the giant tin-can buildings. Four of the airmen rode herd behind, the others went elsewhere.

Footsteps echoed in the cavernous building. Rawhide Robinson's high-heeled boots clicked as he put one sore foot in front of the other attempting to keep pace. Coming from bright sunlight into the dim building made it difficult to see what there was to see, but he sensed the space was mostly empty.

The parade approached a wall and stopped before a large metal door split down the middle. The sergeant pushed a black button on the wall beside the door and stood with hands clasped behind his back. Rawhide Robinson studied a light above the door—a glass ball in a wire cage glowed bright, but he could see no flame, nor hear the hiss of gas nor smell coal oil. High up, near the middle of the curved roof, he noticed a row of similar, but larger, gadgets spaced along the length of the building.

A bell dinged and the double doors slid apart revealing a small room with plain walls. The sergeant stepped into the room and about-faced. One of the airmen shoved the cowboy inside and followed him in along with the three others. Rawhide Robinson's eyes widened when the doors slid shut. The sergeant pushed a button on a panel, causing a jolt to the room, and the perplexed cowboy's stomach flip-flopped when the floor dropped. No one else appeared frightened at the turn of events, so he swallowed hard and rode it out. After a few moments that seemed like several hours, the confined quarters came to a shuddering stop and the doors slid apart, revealing a whole different place than when they slid shut.

Again, a shove in the back propelled the knock-kneed cowboy through the doors. A long, narrow hallway pointed off to either side. Marching along on the ceiling were other light fixtures the like of which Rawhide Robinson had never seen—long tubes that cast a sickly glow. The light reflected off a gray and white checkerboard floor. Everything else was painted a putrid shade of green that looked admirable on rabbitbrush, but on the long swathes of the walls and ceiling was nearly as nauseating as the ride in the room that brought him here.

Again, marching feet echoed as the sergeant led the way down the hallway. The wall on one side was uninterrupted, along the opposite wall marched doors at regular intervals, all painted the same shade of repugnant green. On the wall beside each of the identical doors was a little sign with an unfathomable combination of letters and numbers.

After walking what felt like three furlongs to the cowboy's hurting hooves, the sergeant opened a seemingly random door. "In here," he said.

Rawhide Robinson walked past the door and it closed behind him. The room offered no relief from the repulsive pale green paint, and the close walls barely accommodated a metal table with a pair of metal chairs on either side. After looking around for a minute, the cowboy tried the door and found it locked. He fiddled with a switch on the wall by the door and discovered it turned the room dark. He fiddled with it some more, and the curious glass ball in its cage on the ceiling shined bright again, off and on, off and on, off and on when he flipped the switch, as if by magic.

Lacking any other amusement in his isolation, the cowboy plopped down into one of the uncomfortable chairs, yawned a big yawn, tipped his thirteen-gallon hat over his eyes, flipped off the light, and settled himself in for a serious bout of snoring.

Chapter Seven

Rawhide Robinson bolted upright and swept back his hat when the door opened and light flooded the room.

He scoured his eyes with his fists and blinked two men into focus. One wore a fancy uniform, the other a wrinkled and rumpled Sunday-go-to-meeting suit. The necks of both men were cinched up tight with neckties. The cowboy fingered the wild rag bandana around his own throat, stretched his neck and swallowed.

The chairs screeched on the hard floor as the men slid them away from the table and took seats opposite Rawhide Robinson. With one eye wide open and the other half shut under a furrowed brow, he studied his guests, looking from one to the other and back again. The military man sat straight and tall, hands folded, fingers interlaced, resting on the tabletop, steely eyes boring holes in the cowboy's forehead. The other man unfolded a stiff paper and shuffled through some papers tucked inside. The cowboy watched him pull a slender cylinder from his shirt pocket, click the button on top, and use the curious instrument to start writing on a sheet of paper. Neither man spoke for several minutes.

Eventually, the man in the suit looked up. He stared at Rawhide Robinson, who refused to flinch at the scrutiny. The man clicked the button on the pen and set it aside, stopped to light a cigarette with a small, shiny silver box he took from a shirt pocket, and said, "Do you have any idea how much trouble you're in?"

Rawhide Robinson said nothing.

"No? Well, let me tell you. You are trespassing on government territory. You have willfully entered a top-secret military facility. We don't know how you got in here, so let's start there."

Rawhide Robinson said nothing.

"No? How about something simple, then." He picked up and clicked the pen again, and readied to write. "Your name?"

Rawhide Robinson said nothing.

The silence grew uncomfortable and was broken when the man in the suit slapped the table top with enough force to bounce it off the floor. "Listen to me, you no-account saddle tramp. Answer the questions, or you'll be subjected to interrogation techniques that are significantly less pleasant. Tell me your name!"

The unruffled military officer still sat quietly, his hands, fingers interlaced, unmoved upon the table. "I suggest you cooperate. Nothing good will happen otherwise."

The other man squished out his cigarette in the ashtray, lit its successor, brushed the ashes from his lapels, clicked his pen a time or two, and prepared again to write.

"My name ain't nothing extra," the cowboy said after a moment. "So, I guess there ain't no harm in saying it. Rawhide Robinson."

The man in the suit laughed as he wrote the name on a form. "Rawhide Robinson? What are you, some kind of comic book hero?"

"Nope. Just an ordinary cowboy. What's a comic book?"

"What are you doing here?"

The cowboy's eyebrows arched upward. "Well, mister, I'm just a-sittin' here in this little room listening to you all make chin music. You oughta could see that your ownself."

The interrogator clicked the button on his pen several times as he tried to stare down the cowboy. It did not work. Rawhide Robinson remained as placid as a springtime morning in the Texas Hill Country.

"What I mean, Mister…" the man paused to consult the paper before him, "…Robinson, is, what were you doing on the base? Before the security police caught you?"

Rawhide Robinson propped an ankle atop the opposite knee and spun the rowel on the spur on the boot heel. When the jingling stopped, he said, "You can call me Rawhide. I don't hold with much 'mistering' and such formal talk."

"Just answer the question, please."

Another spin of the spur rowel. "Just doing my job. Hunting for cows."

"Cows! Cattle have not been allowed on this property for years—not since the base was established well over a decade ago!"

This time, Rawhide Robinson's eyebrows wrinkled downward. "Well, I guess maybe the cows don't know it," he said as he gave the rowel another spin.

"The ranchers know it. They've cooperated with the Air Force all along."

Another spin. "Well, fellers, all I know is that old man Elizondo over at the 51 Ranch sent me out this way to check on his cows. Leastways his straw boss, Matt Brooks, did. It ain't nothin' I ain't done before, same as other brush poppers did before me, and same as other hands will do as long as there's cows to take care of."

The men looked aghast at the cowboy, looked at one another, and looked back at the cowboy. The interrogator clicked his pen as he stared, then set to scratching words on a paper as fast as he could drag ink across the page. He set the pen aside, stubbed out his cigarette, slid the papers into the folder, nodded at the man in uniform, and the pair of them rose as if attached to the same set of strings and left the room, closing the door behind them.

For a moment, Rawhide Robinson stared at the closed door. He tried the knob and found the door locked. There was no sound, save the distant echo of retreating footsteps. The cowboy lifted his lid, raked his fingers through his hair and sat back down. He picked up the left-behind pen, studied it from end to end, pushed the button at the top and watched the business end of the curious writing instrument click in and out.

He slipped the pen into a vest pocket for safekeeping, where it nestled among strips of whang leather, a tally book with a stub of pencil, a Barlow knife, and a waterproof tube of matches. If the man in the suit who left it behind came back, he would return it. Surely such an instrument was valuable.

Again, Rawhide Robinson turned off the light, hunkered down in his chair, tipped it back against the wall, and proceeded to examine the insides of his eyelids in case there might be some clue concerning his present situation engraved there. He soon tired of the inspection and fell asleep.

The door did not awaken him when next it opened, for the man who opened it did so slowly, and stood in the half-light listening to the soft snoring of the cowboy. Finally, he switched on the light and waited.

Rawhide Robinson sensed the change in circumstances even through the filter of the crown of his thirteen-gallon hat. Without moving otherwise, he reached into his vest pocket, felt around for the pen and held it up. "Lookin' for this?" he muffled from under the hat.

"Sorry?"

The unfamiliar voice brought the cowboy fully awake. He tipped the chair forward and swept back his hat. The man, now sitting across the table, wore a white shirt like the man in the suit. But he wore no jacket and the sleeves of the shirt were rolled nearly to his elbows, and, rather than a necktie, he wore a bow tie.

The cowboy again proffered the pen. "Last feller who was in here left this behind," he said. "Meant to save it for when I saw him again. Could be you'll see him first."

"Keep it," the man said with a wave of his hand. "They ship them in by the gross. Government issue." He pulled a pipe and tobacco pouch out of his shirt pocket and filled the pipe, then sucked it to life with the aid of a Zippo lighter—same as the shiny silver box the other man used. Rawhide Robinson wondered at the flame that jumped out of the shiny little box, his eyes glued to its gleam until it snapped shut and went back into the pocket with the pouch. The man puffed away, filling the room with sweet-smelling smoke.

"So," he finally said. "You're a cowboy."

Rawhide Robinson nodded.

"Work for the 51 Ranch?" he said after another puff.

Another nod.

"Who runs the place?"

Rawhide Robinson started to speak but coughed softly from the smoke. He cleared his throat. "Dominique Elizondo."

"And Mister Elizondo sent you out here to check on his cattle."

Rawhide Robinson nodded. "He did. His straw boss gave the orders, but it's all the same."

The man sucked on his pipe for a moment. "When did this happen, exactly?"

"Can't rightly say. Time seems to have gotten away from me. Must have been yesterday—day before, maybe."

Another pause. Another puff.

"Tell me, Mister Robinson—"

"—Rawhide, if you please—"

"—Rawhide—this may seem a strange question, but who is the President of the United States?"

Rawhide Robinson pursed his lips. "That's a tough one."

"It is?"

"I don't pay much attention to politics and such, you see. Let me think. As I recall, it's that Yankee General, U.S. Grant—no, wait, come to think of it he might be done and someone else has got the job. Can't say for sure. If it is somebody else, I couldn't tell you his name."

The man seemed to consider that as he puffed on his pipe. "How did you get here—onto the base, I mean?"

"Horseback, of course."

"Horseback? You didn't drive?"

"No. I rode. Why?"

"Where is your horse?"

"Couldn't say. Jugheaded beast must have wandered off in the storm."

"Storm? What storm?"

Rawhide Robinson drew back and furrowed his brow. "Why, that gullywasher we had."

"When?"

Again, the furrowed brow. "Like I said, I'm a mite confused as to time—yesterday, maybe the day before. I reckon so, anyway."

"I don't recall a storm. In fact, I don't believe it has rained here for at least a month."

The man asked more and more questions that confused the cowboy more and more. He asked about Rawhide Robinson's work, his travels, his adventures. He poked. He prodded. He refilled and relit his pipe repeatedly.

Then, "Miste—Rawhide—it has been a pleasure talking with you." He stepped into the hallway, leaving the door ajar. The cowboy heard him say, "Airman, escort this man upstairs. Tell your sergeant I said to drive him to the back gate and turn him loose—with a stern warning."

Chapter Eight

The sun was down by the time the Air Force Security Police airman found the proper key among the many, many on a ring the size of a coiled-up lariat. His two partners took turns offering advice, arguing over the right key, and grabbing the keyring from one another's hands. Once they figured it out and got the job done and the metal gate slammed shut with Rawhide Robinson on the opposite side, the cowboy tipped his hat to the airmen and watched them wheel their noisy vehicle around and roar away.

Headquarters—such as it was—of the 51 Ranch was yet miles away toward the town of Alamo. Lacking any reasonable alternative, the footsore cowboy put one blistering boot in front of the other and repeated the process as hastily and often as discomfort allowed. As dusk deepened, doves cooed, ravens cawed, quail clicked. Coyotes yipped in the distance as lizards scurried across the cooling gravel road the cowboy followed.

Then all went silent.

Rawhide Robinson stopped. He cocked an ear and turned this way and that listening for a clue for the cause of the quiet. Somewhere to the north, he heard it—an engine, similar to those that propelled the airmen's machines, but smaller, higher-pitched. As the noise increased, he saw a light behind the hills, jumping up and down. It crested a hill and the engine and light faded as the machine that made them dropped into another depression. The cowboy, animated by curiosity, hustled ahead toward the place the road and the screaming contraption would intersect.

It looked kind of like one of those bicycles, those wheels he had seen from time to time. But this thing was both more massive and compact—the wheels weren't so high, but more substantial looking; the frame shorter but heavier. Then there was that infernal engine and the bright lights—not just the white one on the front blinding him, but a red one on the tail.

The machine roared up the road bank onto the gravel mere feet away from the spellbound cowboy, so entranced by the sight he lacked the ability to get out of the way. He did manage to step aside in time to avoid the machine as it skidded, fell to its side, and slid past him in the gravel. Skidding along behind, screaming like a stuck pig, was the kid who, seconds before, had been riding astride.

Grinding to a halt, the machine's motor chugged and coughed and died. The rider scrambled to his feet. "What the heck! You crazy? You tryin' to get killed?

You tryin' to kill me?" he hollered as he brushed dirt and gravel off his person. "Look at that," he said, shoving an elbow into the cowboy's face. "I'm bleeding!"

Rawhide Robinson studied the wound in the glow of the thingamajig's lights. "Aw, no need to fuss. Just scraped the bark off is all."

"What are you doin' standin' here in the middle of the road?"

"What are you doing rip-snorting along on that infernal machine without watching where you're going?"

The kid bowed his head and shoved his hands in his pants pockets and scratched at the gravel with his foot. The cowboy could hardly hear "Sorry" when he said it.

"That's all right, kid. I shoulda got out of the way. It don't look like there's any harm done—if that contraption of yours ain't hurt. What is it, anyway?"

"Huh?"

"That thing you was ridin' on. What is it?"

The kid drew back to study the source of such a silly question. What he saw was a cowboy. Not much different from the ones he saw all the time, but not quite the same, either. Given the fact the man was wearing chaps and spurs, he figured he must have been horseback but lost his horse somehow.

"Heck, Mister, it's a motorcycle."

"Motorcycle?"

"Yeah. A Honda 90, y'know."

"Honda? You mean like the knot that makes a loop in a lariat?"

The kid drew back again. "What is it you're doing way out here, Mister. Where's your horse?"

"Can't say. Guess he must've run off in the rainstorm. I'll be takin' it up with him when I see him again. Prob'ly back at the ranch eatin' hay."

The two watched each other warily—more out of curiosity than fear. It was the kid who spoke next.

"You never said what you're doing out here. I don't hardly ever see anyone out here, y'know. Where you going?"

"Just makin' my way back to the ranch."

"What ranch?"

"The 51."

"51? I ain't heard of that one."

Rawhide Robinson pulled off his thirteen-gallon hat and scratched his head. "How can that be? The 51's one of the biggest outfits in these parts. Headquarters can't be too far from here—it's just a ways outside of Alamo."

"I know where Alamo is—that's where I live. But I don't know about no ranch called the 51."

The cowboy inspected the inside of the crown of the hat in his hands as if something in there would make sense of all this confusion, but no answer presented itself. He plopped the hat back on his muddled head and said, “What’s your name, son?”

“Eric. Eric Harris. What’s yours?”

“Rawhide Robinson is what I go by. Rawhide ain’t my real name, of course, but it’s been so long since I used it I don’t rightly remember what it was.”

Eric laughed. He hefted the motorbike upright, a job that was almost beyond his ability. Propping it on its kickstand, he walked around it checking for damage. He fingered the scratches in the paint on the side of the gas tank, gave the handlebars a shake, and wiggled and wobbled the front wheel. Swinging a leg over, he toed out the kickstarter pedal, gripped the hand clutch and stepped down on the starter. It took three tries and some twisting of the gas feed on the handgrip, but the engine spit and sputtered and came to life. The kid revved the engine repeatedly as the cowboy cringed, and, deciding it sounded healthy enough, let it idle.

“Is it all right?” Rawhide Robinson said. “Anything messed up on it?”

“Nah, it’s okay.” He heeled up the kickstand and stared at the cowboy. “So what you gonna do, Mister Rawhide Robinson?”

“Don’t rightly know, Eric.”

"Get on," the kid said, revving the motorbike's engine. "I'll give you a ride to Alamo."

Although known far and wide as a cowboy who could ride anything with hair on, Rawhide Robinson's first thought was that this contraption, this machine, this gadget, this motorcycle, didn't grow hair. He was skeptical. Doubtful. Tentative. Reluctant. Disinclined. Hesitant. Uncertain. Wavering. Unsure. Diffident. Indisposed. Loath. Balky.

The fact is, Rawhide Robinson was afraid.

But, in keeping with the code of life that was The Cowboy Way, Rawhide Robinson pulled his hat down over his ears as if about to board a salty bronc, swung a leg across the motorcycle, wiggled around to familiarize his seat with the seat, and said, "Let 'er rip!"

Chapter Nine

The man in the rumpled suit trembled. His florid face quivered. His fists shook. An explosion looked imminent.

"You turned him loose!?" he hissed through clenched teeth. "You let him go?!" he said, louder this time. "He's gone!?" he shouted with sufficient force to rattle the windows—had there been any windows.

The uniformed officer stood by, hands clasped behind his back, watching his CIA colleague's ire pummel the psychiatrist.

"What the #@&% were you thinking, Doc!?" the man in the suit hollered, stepping toward the shrink, who let the anger wash over him without effect.

"Take it easy," the military officer said. "This won't get us anywhere. Doctor, his questions are legitimate. Would you care to enlighten us?"

"Sit down," the doctor said.

His guests took the two chairs opposite the desk in his cramped office. The psychiatrist closed the file folder on his desk, unlocked a file drawer and stuffed it inside, and let the retractable key ring zip back into its casing clipped to his belt. He leaned back in his chair and laced his fingers behind his head. "What's the big deal, gentlemen?"

Still appearing on the verge of apoplexy, the CIA man jerked loose his tie and thumbed loose the collar button. "The man was an intruder!" he hissed. "Lacking a thorough investigation, we can't be sure what he was doing here. We don't know where he came from, how he got here, who sent him, what he was looking for…." His voice trailed off, and he slumped back into his chair, exhausted.

The psychiatrist said, "Well, gentlemen, suffice it to say that cowboy doesn't know the answers to those questions any more than you do. He's harmless."

The Air Force officer, sitting at attention in his chair, said, "You seem convinced, Doctor. How can you be sure?"

The doctor leaned forward, arcing his arms forward until his laced fingers rested on the desk. "The man is crazy."

"Is that a medical diagnosis, Doc?" the CIA man spat.

"Absolutely. He's stark raving mad. Loony as a goose. Nutty as a fruitcake. Off his nut. Off his rocker. Crazy as a bedbug. He's got a screw loose. Do you get my drift?"

The intelligence agent offered no response.

When the silence became uncomfortable, the military man cleared his throat. “Why do you think so?”

Returning to his semi-reclined position, the doctor explained the cowboy’s confusion. “He swears he works on the 51 Ranch. That place was bulldozed when the government ran off all the miners and ranchers back in ’55. Not that there was much left of the place by then. He claimed he worked for Dom Elizondo—”

“—Who?”

“Dominique Elizondo. He was the Basque rancher that started the 51 back in the nineteenth century. Didn’t own much, really. Ran his cows on the open range—wherever they could find a bite to eat between here and Alamo. Died in 1905, 1906, somewhere around there. Left the place to his daughter, who left it to her son, who didn’t keep the place up. Fact is, he was happy when the government moved in. Paid him more than the place was worth. I understand he drank up the money and died down in Las Vegas a few years ago. So, one thing’s for certain—that cowboy is seriously confused. Must’ve read a history of Lincoln County or something. But there’s no way he worked for the 51.

“Rumor has it, by the way, that the old 51 Ranch is why the government named this place Area 51.”

The Air Force officer ruminated for a minute. "Anything else about the cowboy that convinces you he is mentally unstable?"

"Oh, yes. For sure. The man's so muddled he has no sense of time. Can't remember when he got here—something to do with a rainstorm, which we haven't had for weeks. Thinks he may have been struck by lightning.

"The man doesn't have the slightest idea what year it is. Says the last President of the United States he remembers is Ulysses S. Grant. Claims he trained camels for the Army down in Texas. Drove a herd of cats to Tombstone. And other cockamamie claims. I tell you, he's harmless. I didn't do a blood draw, but it wouldn't surprise me to find he's circulating about ninety proof."

The men soaked that up for a while. The CIA man, now looking less likely to burst into flame, said, "How do you think he got here, Doc?"

"Beats me. Maybe he dropped out of one of those flying saucers folks swear you people are hiding out here."

*****

The call came the next day. A message awaited the psychiatrist when he finished a counseling session with a pilot. The elevator took him up four levels where he was to report to a conference room. Only the signs signaled this level was any different than any other. The same pale green paint covered every surface save the floor, which featured the same gray and white tile that paved the entire facility.

He knocked when he located the designated door. He listened as the lock turned from within. An airman, wearing the dark blue Security Police helmet, ushered him inside, through the vestibule, and through another door into the meeting room.

The military man was there, seated at attention in his dress uniform. Beside him sat the CIA agent, his collar unbuttoned and tie loosened, suit jacket rumpled. His hair was askew from repeated rakings with his fingers and dark whiskers shadowed along his jawline. Patches, as dark as the whiskers, encircled his eyes.

Also in the room were two men in white lab coats, one young, the other middle-aged. Each wore a Van Dyke beard as if it were part of a uniform. The younger man wore thick glasses with heavy black frames; a cigarette dangled from the older man's lip and filter-tipped butts filled an ashtray on the table.

Scientists, the doctor thought.

"Doctor, thank you for joining us," the military man said. "Please, sit."

He did.

"These men are from one of our contractors. Physicists. They are interested in what you have to say about the cowboy."

With furrowed brow, the doctor inspected the physicists, looked at the intelligence agent, then the Air Force officer. "I have nothing to add," he said. "You have my written report. The explanation I gave yesterday has not changed."

"Yes, Doctor. But, as you can imagine, our investigation is ongoing. Keep in mind that the trespasser witnessed the approach and landing of an aircraft that, according to the government of the United States of America, does not exist. We are compelled to get to the bottom of this situation. As part of our inquiries, these men have a few questions for you."

The psychiatrist pulled out a chair at the end of the government-issue conference table. The older of the scientists offered introductions and when names and titles were exchanged, the three civilians nodded acknowledgement.

"Doctor," one said.

"Doctor," the other said.

"Doctor," the psychiatrist replied with a nod. "How can I be of assistance?"

The middle-aged scientist lit a cigarette and asked the psychiatrist to relate the cowboy's report of how he came to be on the base.

The psychiatrist filled and lit his pipe, snapped the silver lid of his lighter shut to douse the flame and dropped it into his shirt pocket. He adjusted his bowtie, unbuttoned his cuffs, and rolled them a couple of turns to expose the lower half of his forearms. He scooted his chair back and crossed his legs, folded his arms, and pointed at the physicists with the stem of his pipe.

"Now, what is it, specifically, you gentlemen want to know?"

The older of the two asked the questions. "This man, this cowboy—you say he believed himself to be somewhere in the nineteenth century."

"He didn't say so, not exactly. But the people and places he recounted were contemporary to that period—more specifically, the late 1870s or the 1880s. Although I could not say so with precision. And keep in mind, he did not make any such claim. He was confused, at best; more likely mentally unbalanced."

The younger physicist kept a government-issue ballpoint pen at work, furiously recording word-for-word as much of the psychiatrist's report as he could and paraphrasing the rest.

"He claimed to be herding cattle?"

"More or less. Said he was riding in the Papoose Range to locate cattle and check their condition."

"So he was on a horse?"

"Yes."

"But he did not know what happened to the horse?"

"No. He assumed it 'spooked and lit a shuck' as he put it, during the storm."

Throughout the questioning, the military man looked on placidly while the CIA man chain-smoked cigarettes and clicked and clicked and clicked the button on a ballpoint pen.

The physicist said, "This storm—what, exactly, did he say?"

"Said he sought shelter under a cedar tree—more likely a mountain juniper, but commonly called a cedar, as you know. The tree offered little cover from the storm, which he said was 'a regular gully washer'—but he saw no alternative protection. The lightning and thunder made the horse skittish, and worried the cowboy as well. Lightning was striking all around, thunder so close he claimed he could feel it. Then there was a flash of light and that's all he remembered."

"Until he woke up?"

"Of course."

"Then what?"

The psychiatrist drew on his pipe as he collected his thoughts. “When he awakened, the storm was gone—without a trace, I might add, he said there was no mud, no sign of dampness anywhere, except his clothing. The sun was shining, the sky clear and blue.”

“He did not find this strange?”

“Of course he did. He found everything strange—‘a latigo hole too slack,’ he said. But he couldn’t quite put his finger on it.”

“And the horse?”

“No sign of it.”

The questions and answers continued. Occasionally, the military man and CIA man in the rumpled suit pitched in, adding details based on what the cowboy told them. They did not believe the cowboy’s explanations. On the other hand, they did not know what to believe. The physicists asked again and again about the lightning strike, hoping to ferret out additional detail—of which there was none to be had.

After studying the notes the younger man had taken, and whispering to one another, and scribbling some sort of equations on the note pad, and whispering some more, the physicists turned to the military man, still sitting at attention in his chair, looking unaffected by the meeting.

"Sir," the older scientist said. "We may have an explanation."

Chapter Ten

The military man waited, betraying, as usual, no emotion. The CIA man in the suit drummed his fingers on the tabletop, forehead furrowed and lips tight. The psychiatrist watched the physicists with a bemused look, eager to hear their explanation for the appearance of Rawhide Robinson on the base. The scientists whispered to one another and tinkered with the equations on the notepad.

The CIA man stopped his fingertip tattoo and pounded the table with his fist. "@#&%+! Will you two eggheads knock it off and tell us what you think!"

Unaccustomed to such outbursts, the physicists' eyes widened as they looked at each other, then at the intelligence officer.

"I'm sorry, gentlemen," the CIA man said. "But that man is still out there. Time is of the essence. We have no idea where he is or who he is talking to or what he is telling them. He could be revealing secrets to our enemies at this very minute."

The psychiatrist laughed.

"What's so funny, Doc? Apparently you do not appreciate the gravity of the situation," the florid-faced

CIA operative said, stubbing out a cigarette and lighting another. As he smoked, he slipped a ballpoint pen from his shirt pocket and incessantly clicked its button.

"You need to let your belt out a notch or you're going to do yourself a damage," the shrink said. "I can assure you, nothing that crazy cowboy says is likely to be believed by anybody."

"You are seriously misreading the threat. If you knew what I know, you would not be so cavalier in your attitude."

"Yeah, right. You spooks are so paranoid I'm surprised you dare go out at all. And by the way, it wouldn't hurt you any to cut back on the cigarettes. You seem a bit obsessed with the ballpoint pen, as well."

The CIA man stood and shook a finger in the doctor's face. "You!— you—!"

"Gentlemen," the military man said. "This is getting us nowhere. Let us, please, remain calm." Then, to the physicists, "If you gentlemen would enlighten us, we would be most grateful."

The older physicist nodded at the younger one, who smoothed the page of his notepad, shoved his spectacles up the bridge of his nose with a forefinger, blinked rapidly, licked his lips, and said, "You are all, I assume, familiar, on some level, with Einstein's theory of general relativity."

He shifted his eyes back and forth from the military man, the CIA man, and the psychiatrist as each nodded in the affirmative.

"Yes, well. One of the lesser-known aspects of that theory, beyond the grasp of physicists, even, is the mathematical prediction of Einstein-Rosen bridges."

Again, he looked to his audience for acknowledgement but saw only blank stares.

"Einstein-Rosen bridges?" he said again, but the void in the countenances of his audience remained.

"Wormholes," the other physicist offered.

"Wormholes?" said the intelligence agent, demonstrating a decided lack of intelligence on the subject.

"Wormholes," said the Air Force officer. "Enlighten us."

The older physicist nodded to the younger physicist, who repeated the smoothing of the page, the adjustment of eyeglasses, and the licking of lips. "Einstein-Rosen bridges, or wormholes," he said, "are, for lack of more precise language, shortcuts through space-time." The young man's words picked up speed as excitement with his subject grew. "Now, they are only theoretical, mind you—science has developed no experimental methods to prove, or disprove, the existence of wormholes. However, mathematical calculations suggest a very real possibility of their occurrence under certain conditions."

"Hmmph," the CIA man grunted, spreading his arms, palms upward, then shouted, "What has this gobbledygook got to do with anything?"

The senior physicist stopped the harangue with a raised hand. "Please. Let him finish."

"Hmmph. Okay. Get to the point."

The scientist started up again. "What it comes down to, in layman's terms, is the possibility of time travel."

All three audience members sat upright—well, the shrink and the spook did, the military man, as usual, already sat at attention.

The young physicist continued. "Should a wormhole open in space-time, predictions say two different points in space-time could be connected by a tunnel of sorts—an entry and exit point joined by a tunnel. It is thought these would be more-or-less spherical in nature. A physical body entering the wormhole could travel across time and distance, for all practical purposes, instantly."

The elder egghead patted his colleague on the back and nodded his approval. "Here's what we think may have—may have—happened. If, in fact, this cowboy of yours was actually struck by lightning, or in the immediate proximity of a strike, it is possible—possible—that the lightning bolt could have—could have—generated enough electromagnetic energy to open a wormhole that enveloped the cowboy at whatever point in space-time he occupied, then spit him out at some other point."

Expelled breath rushed into the room as the men remembered respiration and its importance to survival. They considered, cogitated, mused, and meditated on what they had just heard.

After what he deemed a suitable interval for introspection, the physicist continued. "Gentlemen, it is possible—unlikely, but possible—that the cowboy was, in fact, caught in a thunderstorm on the Papoose Range sometime in days gone by, as he claimed. But, thanks to a bolt of lightning, found himself thrust, involuntarily, into our day and time."

Another long pause ensued as the military man, intelligence agent, and psychiatrist considered the scientists' explanation—possible explanation. And how it would, should, or could affect future actions. No one of them, it is safe to say, had any experience with responding to the possibility of a time-traveling cowboy who witnessed sights and sounds deemed off limits to ordinary citizens.

"Gentlemen," the Air Force officer said after a time, "please share your opinions on this matter in light of this information. Doctor?"

"I don't see this as affecting the situation in any way vis-à-vis the base or the government. I am concerned for the well-being of the cowboy. The possibility of time travel certainly sheds light on his confusion."

The man in the suit stubbed out his cigarette, smashing the butt to smithereens in the process, and spilling other butts onto the tabletop. "We've got to catch him! This cockamamie 'wormhole' nonsense changes nothing!"

"What?" the shrink said. "How can you say that?"

"He saw things he ought not to have seen! He knows things that he, and everyone else outside the fence, has no business knowing!"

"Oh, come on! He doesn't know a darn thing—he doesn't even know what year it is."

"So what? He saw the plane."

"He doesn't even know what an airplane is!"

The CIA man shook a cigarette from his pack and fired it up with his lighter and traded the Zippo for the ballpoint and its click. "That may make it worse. It could mean his explanations, his descriptions, will be all the more detailed. He could pass along secrets concerning our technology without even knowing it," he said with a click of his pen.

"And just who is he going to tell?"

"It could be anybody! You know there are always nutcases hanging around Alamo; weirdos sitting on every hilltop on the perimeter with binoculars and cameras with telephoto lenses. Any one of them could be a Soviet spy!"

"Oh, give it a break," the psychiatrist said as he knocked the dottle out of his pipe and dropped it stem first into his shirt pocket. "You said it yourself—most of the people lurking about out there are nutcases and weirdos. Even if they did happen to talk to the cowboy, they'd think he was crazier than they are. He wouldn't be taken seriously."

"So you say! I say we've got to keep him from talking. We've got to find that cowboy."

The Air Force officer kneaded his chin and looked from the CIA man in the rumpled suit to the psychiatrist to the physicists and back again. "Gentlemen," he said, "I am inclined to agree that we should find this cowboy."

"Excellent!" the physicists said, as if coached to exclaim in unison. The older one said, "We would relish an opportunity to question him concerning the lightning strike and its aftereffects. His experience has important ramifications for science." The younger egghead perked up. "We could publish a paper!"

"Hold on," said the CIA man, clicking his pen for emphasis. "Not a word of this goes anywhere! This incident, whatever its nature proves to be, will be classified at the highest level of secrecy. Not a word!" He stubbed out his cigarette and leaned back in his chair.

"Be that as it may," the military man said, "I think it best to get this cowboy back here until we decide what to do. However, I do not think it would be in our best interest to launch a manhunt. Dispatching teams of uniformed airmen and security police in a wide-area search would only invite questions we would rather not have asked. I want this to be low profile."

The man in the suit smiled. "Not to worry, Sir. My men can handle it."

"Oh, great," the shrink said. "Spooks in suits. That shouldn't arouse suspicion."

Chapter Eleven

Rawhide Robinson rode with stiff legs thrust forward, one hand atop his thirteen-gallon hat, the other around Eric's waist. Wind whipped his eyelashes and whistled in his ears. The scream of the motorbike's engine masked all other sound. From time to time he tipped his head to one side or the other, and through squinted eyes tried to see whatever the headlight beam illuminated. The rest of the world was lost in darkness, save the occasional jackrabbit that joined them on the road for brief intervals or the sagebrush that lined the gravel road. Once, when rounding a bend in the road, the headlight revealed the decrepit remains of a corral.

"Eric," the cowboy said. "Can you stop this thing?"

The boy throttled down the engine and stopped, struggling to keep the Honda upright. "Put your feet down!" he said.

The reluctant rider did so, then stood and stepped backward off the bike. "Can you shine your light over there?" he said, pointing at the corral.

As the boy wheeled around, Rawhide Robinson walked back to the wrecked pen. There was something familiar about the old round corral. Most of the stout cedar posts still stood, some of the top and bottom cross planks were intact, a few others sagged or dangled from the posts. An upright board still stood here and there, but most looked to have been pulled loose. The ring of smoke-blackened rocks in the corral suggested the wood had fed bonfires. Tin cans were scattered about, along with other assorted litter.

As his eyes adjusted to the darkness, and as he instructed Eric to redirect the light, Rawhide Robinson walked past the corral and studied a jumble of hewn stones outlining what was once the foundation of a building. He slipped his hands in his hind pockets and wagged his head.

"This is it," he said.

"What?"

"Headquarters of the 51 Ranch."

Eric said nothing.

"You sure you don't remember nothing else being here?"

"No Sir. Just what's here. Like this. I've been out here with my friends sometimes. Weenie roasts, or sleeping out, y'know. High school kids, they come out here to party sometimes. All them beer cans, y'know."

The cowboy shook his head again, not understanding half of what the boy was saying. "It's gone. All of it." He stood, looking around.

“We better go. It’s late. Mom’ll be worried. Or fit to kill me.”

Seeing no alternative in the waste that was once his place of employment, Rawhide Robinson slid back onto the Honda’s seat.

The ride on into Alamo was equally hair-raising for the cowboy. The fact that he had forked more recalcitrant broncs than he could remember, or survived numerous other adventures and exploits that ranked much higher on the danger scale, did not assuage his discomfort at hightailing it down a gravel road in the dark aboard a motorbike.

They topped a rise and Rawhide Robinson peeked around Eric and saw the lights of the town spread out before him. The place bore no resemblance to the Alamo he knew. His jaw dropped in wonder, but he slammed it shut in a hurry, fearing a feast of flying insects.

The cowboy had, of course, seen city lights before. He had witnessed glowing light from every window in Dodge City when a trail herd hit town. He had seen San Antonio shining on a Saturday night. And he had marveled at seemingly endless rows of streetlights in Chicago during visits there. But those other lights—from candles, gas flames, coal-oil lanterns and the like—dimmed in comparison to the sparkle, the shimmer, the glitter, the gleam on the small town of Alamo. His wonderment at the luminosity inflated as they rode into town. *Land sakes*, he thought, *a man could stand in the middle of the street at midnight and read a dime novel! If he was so inclined, a feller could write a letter of an evening without a candle catching his eyebrows on fire!*

Eric slowed the motorbike, the engine running at a relatively quiet idle. "Gotta take it easy in town," Eric said. "Watch out for the town clown, y'know."

"Town clown?"

"Cop. Policeman, y'know. We ain't got but one and mostly he leaves us alone with our motorcycles, but y'never know."

"Why would he care?"

"I ain't got a license. I'm only fourteen and you can't get a driver's license till you're sixteen, y'know."

"You need a license 'fore you can drive one of these outfits?"

"Sure."

"How 'bout them other things I seen—four-wheeled outfits, like a buggy."

"Well, yeah…."

They crossed what the cowboy figured must be the main street—it was wider and covered with macadam or something else that made it hard, and fringed here and there with business establishments. Beyond that, it was back onto unpaved streets lit only by beams leaking out of house windows and streetlights at the corners. Still, Rawhide Robinson thought, the town was brighter than any he had seen in all the nights of his life.

After a few turns and corners, they followed a street to its end. At the last house, dark save for a bright light above a side door, the motorbike turned into the driveway. Eric idled the bike around to the back of the house and shut it off. The cowboy stood and stepped back off the seat as Eric pushed down a kickstand and yanked backward with both hands to lift the Honda onto the prop.

The boy stared at the house for a moment or two, and said "Looks like Mom's not home." He shrugged his shoulders. "C'mon," he said, and walked around the corner of the house and through the lighted side door. He flipped a switch and illuminated a small kitchen.

The cowboy studied the layout. He recognized the sink, figured out what must be the stove, and wondered at a tall white box in the corner with the word "Kelvinator" across the front in silver letters. A table and two chairs sat next to the opposite wall.

Eric said, "Hungry?"

"My belly button's been bouncin' off my backbone since I climbed on that contraption of yours."

The boy fetched a jar of peanut butter and another of jelly from the cupboard, and a loaf of sliced bread from a box on the counter near the refrigerator. "P-B-and-J okay?" He dropped the makings on the table and got a table knife from a drawer.

Rawhide Robinson looked on as Eric pulled two slices of bread from a white plastic bag decorated with red, yellow, and blue spots. He twisted the lids off the jars, stabbed the knife into one of the jars and spread a gooey substance, about the consistency of axle grease but light brown in color, on the bread. The cowboy had no idea what it was and the smell of it did not help. The boy then scooped some dark purple goop from the other jar—Rawhide figured it must be some kind of jam or preserve—and slathered it over the stuff on the bread and slapped the slices together.

"Thought you were hungry," Eric said around a mouthful of the sandwich.

"What is that you're eating?"

"P-B-and-J!"

"I heard that. But what is it you put on them slices of bread?"

"P-B-and-J—peanut butter and jelly, y'know."

"Peanuts? You mean like goobers?"

The boy laughed.

"Ain't nothin' funny about goobers. Goober peas is what they call peanuts, mostly, where I come from."

Eric laughed again. "Not around here. A 'goober' is what comes out of your nose. You wouldn't want to eat no goober."

"How 'bout that purple stuff?"

"Grape jelly."

Rawhide Robinson watched the boy wolf down the sandwich and decided the stuff must be edible. He followed Eric's lead in building a sandwich and took a tentative bite. "Not bad," he said.

The bread sack dwindled to near empty before man and boy were sated. Sometime during the gorge, Eric got a bottle of milk out of the refrigerator.

"Cold! I reckon that must be an icebox over there," Rawhide Robinson said, gesturing toward the white Kelvinator with his glass.

"It's a fridge."

At the cowboy's blank look he added, "Y'know, refrigerator."

Rawhide Robinson shrugged, and drained off the glass.

Eric gathered the supper makings off the table, uncovering a note from his mother in the process.

Gone to the city. Home before dark. Love, Mom

Eric read the note, checked the clock on the wall, read the note aloud. He looked at Rawhide Robinson, and back at the note.

"Mom's never late."

Chapter Twelve

Rawhide Robinson opened his eyes and looked around. It took a minute, but he eventually realized where he was. But the realization did nothing to relieve the anxiety—in fact, it made it worse.

He sat up and swung his legs off the sofa. The newspaper still sat on the floor where he dropped it the night before. Ever since waking up after the storm in the desert he knew something was amiss but could not figure it out to his satisfaction. While he was never much for keeping track of time according to a calendar, the date on the newspaper suggested he was nearly a hundred years away from where he belonged.

Daylight offered the first clear view of the house. Like most of the rest of the world he had been looking at of late, most everything seemed familiar, yet different. This house the boy Eric lived in looked to have more than its share of furniture, at least compared to what the cowboy was accustomed to. The threadbare condition of most of it, however, was little different than the castoff accoutrements in the bunkhouses where he habitually spooled out his bedroll.

Other items—like the fancy white icebox thingamajig in the kitchen—were beyond his ken. The focal point of the living room where he sat was a box about two feet to the side with a glass front and a row of dials and knobs and a strange word—Sylvania—in the corner below the row of knobs. Just what the box might accomplish, he could not imagine. Then there were the light fixtures all over the place. The glowing glass globes hung from the ceiling, topped stands on the floor, and sat on fancy pedestals on tables. By now he had figured out the switches—sometimes on the gadget itself, other times stuck on walls—that lit them, but he knew not how or why they worked.

As he sat contemplating this strange, new world Eric wandered into the room in t-shirt and boxer shorts, bleary-eyed and scratching himself. "You *are* here," he said through a yawn. "Thought maybe I only dreamed about you, y'know." He yawned again, then his eyes snapped wide open and he stood upright. "Mom!" he said, and rushed from the room. Rawhide Robinson heard a door open and, a moment later, close.

Eric hastened back into the living room. "She ain't here!"

Seeing the boy's fear, the cowboy said, "Everything'll be all right, probably, Eric. That paper you had—where's it say she went?"

"The city—Las Vegas. We used to live there. She goes there sometimes to shop, y'know." He swallowed hard. "But she always comes back when she says."

"Well, son, if you think it might be somethin' serious, maybe we ought to go see that policeman you talked about—the 'town clown' you said."

Eric nodded.

"Get your britches on and we'll go look him up. Town this size, he can't be too hard to find."

"No. I'll call him."

Rawhide Robinson looked flummoxed. He pictured the boy stepping out the door into the morning, hollering to the points of the compass through cupped hands. *Well, if that's the way they do things these days, who am I to argue.*

He followed Eric into the kitchen. The boy picked up a black handle thing with round, flat, knobby things on the end, hooked by a coiled twine to a black box stuck on the wall where it had been hanging. He stuck one end up to his ear, then poked his finger into one hole after another on a wheel-like deal on the box and spun it around and back a few times. He stood with the other piece still stuck to his ear. "Is the chief there? Mister Argyle?" he said after a minute.

Rawhide Robinson looked around to see if someone else had come into the room, but it appeared Eric was talking to himself.

"It's Eric. Eric Harris…."

"Yeah. Y'know, Karen Harris's boy…."

"It's my mom—she's gone. I mean, she ain't here. Went to town sometime yesterday and her note said she'd be back by dark, but she ain't come home yet…."

"Yeah, over on Frehner Road…."

"Yeah, okay," Eric said and hung up the phone. He looked at Rawhide Robinson, whose worried face looked back at him. "What?"

"I'm just a little worried, boy—you actin' like you're talking to somebody in that box. It's a mite worrisome."

Eric laughed, despite his anxiety. "You've seen a telephone before, ain't you?"

The cowboy shook his head.

"It's a telephone. You can talk to anybody, anywhere, y'know. Even long distance."

The cowboy thought a moment. "So that was that policeman you was talkin' to? Chief, you called him?"

"Yeah. That's what some people call him. His name's Lamar Argyle. He's the chief of police, I guess—but in our police department, we got a chief, but no Indians, y'know."

Rawhide Robinson found what looked like a coffee-pot on the back of the stove and Eric showed him how to make coffee in a percolator. Breakfast was a P-B-and-J replay. About the time the sandwiches were laid to rest, an automobile pulled up at the side of the house.

"I reckon I'll wait in the other room," Rawhide Robinson said. "I got no reason to meet no lawman just now." He stepped through the doorway into the living room and sat in a stuffed chair in the farthest corner.

"C'mon in," Eric answered the knock at the door.

"Smells like coffee," the policeman said.

Eric looked at the pot on the stove. "Uh, yeah.... You want some?"

The lawman looked at Eric. What're you doin' makin' coffee, boy? Ain't you a bit young for that?"

Eric took a deep breath, hoping an answer would come in with the draft of air. "No—I mean, yes. I mean, I don't drink it. I make it for Mom, y'know. Habit, I guess.... Anyway, you want some? I already got it made."

"Sure, boy. Pour me a cup and tell me the deal with your mother."

Although in another room with a wall between him and the conversation in the kitchen, the house was small enough that Rawhide Robinson could hear every word said.

Eric showed the policeman the note, who opined that it might be too soon to worry. Suggested car trouble, or a prolonged visit with friends. The boy was having none of it, insisting his mother always made it home on time, or informed him of any delay. He insisted his mother had no friends in Las Vegas; at least none she would spend the night with.

Chief Argyle thought for a moment. "What about family?"

"Nope. Well, she does but they don't have anything to do with her, y'know."

"Why's that?"

The boy struggled for an answer. "I don't really know. I know it's something to do with my Dad. Back before I was even born."

"So your ma and her folks don't get along?"

"I guess not. But not really. They don't even talk, y'know. I ain't never met them."

"You think that's got something to do with this?"

Eric had no answer.

The two sat staring at one another across the table. The chief walked to the stove and refilled his coffee mug, then turned and leaned against the stove. "Listen, son, there's something you ain't telling me. And if I don't know what's going on here, I can't help you."

Chapter Thirteen

Karen Harris heaved a sigh as the shopping cart clattered and rattled down the grocery store aisle. The left front wheel hit the ground only occasionally and when it did, it spun in circles, contributing more to the cart's shimmy, shake, and sway than to its forward motion. The wobbly wagon, heaped with household goods and foodstuffs, shuddered to a stop at the dairy case and Karen hefted two gallon jugs of milk into the cart. When she got home, Eric would consume that milk, and more, before it had time to chill in the fridge. She checked her list and wheeled the cart around with the checkout counter across the market in her sights.

That's when she saw him.

Only a few feet away, Carlo Carlucci scrutinized the bricks of cheese he held, studying one, then the other, then again. Karen hoped to slip past him, but the clang and jangle of the cart as she pushed it into motion caught his attention. He looked at the cart. He looked at her. Their eyes locked.

"Hey!" he said.

With a heave, Karen shoved the cart past him and watched him over her shoulder as she hurried down the aisle. Carlucci glanced at the cheeses, tossed them back into the bin, and loped off down the aisle after the lurching cart. He grabbed the handle and slowed it to a stop. The woman tried to push on, but he held fast. She sagged as the breath left her body in resignation.

"Karen! Long time no see!"

Her look all but withered the lettuce in her cart. "Not long enough."

"Where you been? What's it been, a couple of years?"

She said nothing. Her knuckles whitened on the cart handle.

"Come along, little lady. We got a lot to talk about." Carlo grabbed Karen's arm and jerked her away from the cart and half-dragged her to the parking lot. He opened the back door of a long, low, and wide black automobile and shoved her inside. The car dipped and swayed as it accelerated onto the Las Vegas street. "Factory air," he said as he slid a knob and flipped a switch, then held up a hand to feel the breeze. "Love it."

The cool air reached the back seat as Karen studied her abductor. He hadn't changed much. Still the same flashy rings on his fingers and gold chains around his throat. The shirt collar layered over the top of the brown knit top-stitched leisure suit looked wide enough to allow him to lift off and fly in the draft from the air conditioner. Same mustache, but his hair was different. Rather than the slicked-back oily look she remembered, he now sported long sideburns and a blow-dried do that covered most of his ears and hung over the back of his collar. She was tempted to poke at his hair to see if the layers of spray that held it hostage would splinter or crack. But she resisted, just as she resisted answering his barrage of questions.

He laughed, but there was no mirth in it. "Not to worry, girl. You'll tell me what I want to know soon enough." Carlo's gold canine tooth glinted as he smiled at her over his shoulder. He turned back to the road and laughed again.

Carlo's apartment overlooked a swimming pool and patio lined with palm trees. Karen caught only a glimpse of it before he pulled heavy drapes closed across a sliding glass door leading to a small balcony. Before she had a chance to take in the layout or furnishings, he shoved her into a small room and slammed the door. With no window to shed light, it took a few minutes for Karen to feel her way around the wall and locate a light switch.

Meant to be a bedroom, it looked like Carlo used the place for storage. Several boxes cluttered one corner, along with items of castoff furniture. Karen dragged an upholstered kitchen chair from the tangle. Its high back was loose, but it would serve. She sat for a moment wondering what to do. Knowing it was wasted effort, she tried the door. A hasp or some other fastener must have held it from the outside. The knob turned and the door rattled but would not open. She slid open closet doors to reveal more boxes. An assortment of clothing, some in plastic dry cleaning bags, filled half the closet rod. Assorted bits of this and that littered the shelf above. Nothing, she noted, that would help get out of this predicament. She curled up on the floor using a folded blanket for a pillow and drifted off into fitful sleep.

The rattle of the door startled her awake. As the door opened, she glanced at her watch and read half-past nine. Carlo gestured with his head for her to follow. She stood, stretched, and stepped into the short hallway just as Carlo disappeared around a corner. She followed him into the living room. Two men sat on either end of the sofa. She recognized one, but did not know his name.

Carlo dragged an overstuffed chair over to face the couch and told her to sit. She looked around the room. The flocked wallpaper in shades of red looked like something that belonged on the wall of a casino. Red shag carpet snarled its way across the floor. A tall table, covered with green felt and surrounded by high wooden chairs upholstered in red stood in the corner. A fancy—

but tacky—light fixture hung from a chain hooked to the ceiling. The man who lived here must like his work, she thought, because much of the décor in his home looked like a gambling parlor.

"Okay, lady," Carlo said. "I talked to the boss, and boy was he happy I found you. Eddie and Spuds here, he sent along to make sure you tell us what we want to know."

Eddie and Spuds—one tall and lean, the other tall and shaped like a potato, stared at her with threatening, tough-guy expressions. She stared back, and decided the looks they employed had been perfected over long hours in front of mirrors.

Carlo Carlucci paced back and forth behind Karen. He stopped mid-stride as if something had just occurred to him, and he dragged the pole lamp standing beside the sofa toward the woman and aimed all three of its cone-shaped shades at her face.

Karen couldn't help but laugh. "You've been watching too many gangster movies, Carlo. Or TV police shows. Do you really think three light bulbs and two goons will make me talk?"

"I'll ask the questions."

"Mind if I use the bathroom first?"

Carlo looked to his goons. Eddie lit a cigarette and snapped his Zippo lighter shut as he inhaled deeply, furrowing his brow in an attempt to look menacing. Spuds shrugged. Carlo grabbed Karen's arm, hoisted her to her feet, and guided her back into the hallway. He reached through the doorway and turned on the bathroom light and pushed her through. "Don't be long."

She could hear him breathing outside the door as she did her business. She flushed and turned the water on in the sink, using the noise to cover the sound as she opened the medicine cabinet. Nothing inside but a can of shaving cream and an unwashed safety razor and a bottle of aftershave lotion on the middle shelf, a frayed toothbrush and mauled tube of toothpaste on the lower shelf. Seeing no help, she closed the cabinet.

"Hurry up in there."

"Give a lady some privacy." Karen jerked the door open assisted by the leaning weight of Carlo, and he stumbled and nearly fell. He stood, straightened his leisure suit jacket with a tug on the tails. "Let's go."

Back on the hot seat, Karen listened as Carlo resumed pacing behind her.

"Where have you been, Karen? Where's your old man? He's the one we want."

She did not answer.

"What have you been doing? It's been nearly two years."

"Minding my own business."

"Don't get smart. The situation you're in, your business is our business."

"Oh? Why's that, Carlo?"

"Like I said, don't get smart. You know that deadbeat husband of yours ain't much of a gambler—leastways not a good one. You know he's into us for more than five large."

"Five large? Large what? What are you talking about?"

"Five large! You know—five grand. Fifty Benjamins. Fifty C-notes. Fifty yards. You know good and well we got chits for five-thousand bucks with your welching hubby's signature on them. Plus interest. The boss says he's waited long enough. He wants his money."

"Well, he won't get it from me. I haven't got that kind of money."

"What about your flyboy husband? Where is he?"

Karen swallowed hard, then laughed. "You won't get it from him, either. He's dead."

"Dead?"

"Dead. His wing shipped out to Vietnam. He got shot down."

Carlo stopped pacing and flopped down on the couch between Spuds and Eddie. He could barely keep his jaw closed—try as he might to avoid it, it kept dropping. He tried to speak several times, but could form no words. After several minutes, he stood again.

Half dragging Karen out of her seat and down the hall, he shoved her into the spare room.

"I gotta go talk to the boss. Don't try anything."

Chapter Fourteen

Eric sat with his hands folded atop the table, staring as if trying to memorize the pattern on the tablecloth. “Honest, Chief Argyle—I don’t know anything more about what’s happened to Mom.”

“I think it might have something to do with your father.”

The boy’s head snapped up and his eyes snapped wide open. “What do you mean? You don’t know nothin’ about Dad.”

The lawman sipped at his coffee, grimaced, and set the mug on the counter. “Fact is, I do.”

“How could you? He never even lived here.”

“I know that, Eric. But when he died—”

Eric jumped to his feet, fists balled. “Shut up! You shut up about him! You don’t know nothing!”

The upset urged Rawhide Robinson to his feet and he walked into the kitchen. The policeman stepped away from the stove and set his hand atop the pistol holstered at his waist. “Hold it right there, Mister. Who the hell are you? What’s your business here?”

The cowboy looked at Eric and saw tears filling his eyes. "You're unsettling the boy. There ain't no need for that."

"I repeat—who are you?"

"Rawhide Robinson's what I go by. I reckon that'll do."

"What are you doing here?"

"I—I guess you'd say I'm a friend of Eric's."

The chief said to the boy, "That so?"

Eric nodded.

"You know anything about Karen being missing?" the lawman said to the cowboy.

"Karen?"

"Eric's mother—looks like if you was a friend of his, like you claim, you'd know that name."

Rawhide Robinson smiled. "Well, we're friends, but we only just met." Then, to Eric, "Son, why don't you leave me to talk to this policeman alone."

Eric looked at the law officer, looked at the cowboy, and back at the policeman, who nodded his permission. The boy went out the door and the men watched him walk across the yard and plop down against the trunk of a shade tree.

The chief eyed Rawhide Robinson, studying him from hat crown to boot heel. "So, mister 'Rawhide

Robinson,' how do I know you haven't got something to do with this?"

"All you got's my word."

"Hmmph. Why should I believe you? You look like nothing more than a shiftless saddle tramp."

The cowboy bristled, raised himself to full height. "I reckon your eyes work just fine, then. I've been punchin' cows since I was a button—and I'm proud to say so."

"Who do you ride for?"

The cowboy hesitated. Then, "I guess you could say I'm out of work just now. I ain't ridin' the grub line yet, but my last cowboyin' job…. Well, it disappeared, I guess you'd say."

Chief Argyle removed his hat and pulled a toothpick from a bunch tucked into the ribbon band. He slipped it between his lips, leaned his backside against the stove, and folded his arms. "What do you know about Karen? Her being missing, I mean."

"Nothin' more than what's been wrote on that piece of paper. Now, how's about you tell me about Eric's pa."

Argyle pulled the toothpick from his mouth and used it to clean his fingernails. "You know anything about him?"

"Not a word."

After scraping at his fingernails for a moment, the policeman said, “I’ve not met the man, myself. Far as I know, he never set foot in Alamo.”

The chief told Rawhide Robinson he first met Karen and Eric under less-than-favorable circumstances. He looked them up after a call from the commanding officer at Nellis Air Force Base outside of Las Vegas, informing him that Dwight Harris’s F-111 fighter aircraft had been blown out of the skies over Vietnam. No parachute deployed and the crew was listed as killed in action. The reluctant policeman became the bearer of bad news, asked to make initial contact with the family. Representatives of the Air Force would visit as soon as practicable.

Later, the policeman said, he got a call from the Las Vegas Police Department. The flyboy Harris, they said, had had a yen for gambling and spent too much of his free time astraddle casino stools. His skill as a gambler did not match his enthusiasm and as a result he had IOUs at several casinos. His favorite gambling hall, the Stardust, held paper adding up to several thousand dollars. The Stardust’s owners had been strong-arming Harris for months. Respite came when his unit was deployed to Southeast Asia. When he shipped out, Karen and Eric, at his urging, left Las Vegas in the dark of night and relocated to Alamo—out of reach, man and wife hoped, of the mobsters who had been harassing Dwight.

When Dwight got shot down within weeks of deployment, Karen hoped the collectors would write his debts off as a loss. But, to be on the safe side, she opted to stay in Alamo. All this happened some two years ago, and Karen and Eric were now entrenched in the community.

"What I'm wondering, Mister Robinson," the policeman said to wrap up the tale, "is if those Mafia goons in Las Vegas somehow tracked Karen down and are leaning on her for the money."

"Mafia?" Rawhide Robinson said. "You mean Mafia like *La Cosa Nostra*? That's a pretty bad bunch."

"La Cosa Nostra. I've heard it called that. Why, have you had dealings with the Mafia?"

"Once. Over in Sicily, where I was one time." A natural and eager raconteur, Rawhide Robinson nearly launched into the tale but thought better of it. "It's a long story and it happened a long time ago. It don't matter no-how, now."

Chief Argyle lifted his Stetson and ran his fingers through his thick mop of salt-and-pepper hair. "Just a theory," he said. "Could be the mob's got nothing to do with it."

"Does Eric know what his daddy had been up to? Or about the Mafia bein' after him?"

"I don't believe so. Far as he knows, his father is a war hero. Which he is. My guess is, Karen had no reason to tell him about the rest. I know I wouldn't."

With that, the chief reset his hat on his head and walked out the door. Rawhide Robinson followed, and they stood and watched the boy sitting under the tree. Eric picked up pebbles from the bare dirt and tossed them at some target only he could see out beyond the scuffed-up toes of his shoes.

Argyle opened the door of his automobile. Rawhide Robinson wondered at the red bubble-like thing on the roof. "I'll call the police in Las Vegas. See if they know anything. I'll let you know if I learn something useful."

Rawhide Robinson nodded and the chief slid onto the car seat and drove away. Eric stood and dusted off his backside and joined the cowboy.

"Eric, where exactly is this place called Las Vegas where your mother went?"

Eric pointed south. "It's down there. 'Bout two hours, I guess."

"Two hours? Can't be far, then. What, ten, maybe fifteen miles?"

The boy laughed. "More like a hundred miles, probably."

The cowboy's forehead furrowed, then relaxed when he smiled. "I get it," he said with a chuckle. "You mean two hours in one of them machines."

"Yeah— y'know, a car. How else?"

Rawhide Robinson didn't answer, lost as he was contemplating a world where a two-hour ride in an automobile amounted to two good days of riding a good horse.

Eric watched the cowboy daydream for a moment, then wakened him with a question. "Why do you want to know about Las Vegas?"

"Why?" Rawhide Robinson said. "I reckon we might have to go there 'fore this is over."

Chapter Fifteen

Nothing. No capture, no sightings, no trail, no trace after two days of looking. The cowboy looked to have disappeared as mysteriously as he appeared. The CIA man climbed out of the open jeep and brushed dust off the shoulders and lapels of his rumpled suit jacket. He picked up one foot then the other, shaking his head at the brown film covering the wingtip shoes and the desert dirt filling the little decorative holes bordering the layers of leather.

Looking around at the other men assigned to the search and their vehicles parked in the complex of metal buildings and other structures on the fringe of Groom Lake, he peeled off the jacket, gave it a shake and tossed it into the jeep. Unbuttoning the cuffs of his limp and wrinkled white shirt, he took a turn or two in each then shoved them further up his forearms.

"Gather 'round," he growled as he flipped open his Zippo lighter and fired up a cigarette. Seven men stepped into a semi-circle around the CIA man. Two, dressed in limp and withered suits nearly identical to the intelligence officer's, left the dark sedan they had been driving. Another suited man stood next to an air force pilot who flew the single-engine search and surveillance plane. The other three were Air Police personnel, one who drove the CIA man around in the jeep, the other two searched in a jeep of their own.

"Just to verify, none of you saw anything…."

One of the suited agents tossed a cigarette butt and ground it into the dirt with a dingy shoe. "We've searched every dirt road, cow path and game trail beyond the back gate. Nothing."

"He didn't just disappear!"

One of the Air Policemen laughed. "Wouldn't surprise me. People'll tell you a lot stranger things have happened at Area 51."

The other men chuckled until interrupted by the CIA man. "That's enough! That cowboy is out there somewhere and we've got to find him before he spreads more stories about this place!"

"All due respect, Sir, where else will we look? For the better part of two days we've covered the country like a blanket—at least as much as possible without drawing attention. We've checked every abandoned mining camp and old shack out there. We've looked under every tree and turned over most of the rocks. There's no sign of him."

Grinding out his smoke on the dusty fender of the jeep, the CIA man shook another from the pack.

"There's only one explanation," he said, pausing to light the cigarette in the fading light. "He must've got a ride into Alamo."

"From who, Sir?" another Air Policeman said. "No one drives those roads except boys on motorbikes or dune buggies. That, and town kids out partying. None of their usual hideouts showed signs of recent activity."

"I don't know. But there's no other explanation. He's got to be in Alamo." After a deep puff on the cigarette, the CIA man blew a cloud of smoke into the evening sky. "You flyboys are dismissed. Thank you for your assistance." The men started off, but stopped to hear, "Oh, and remember—this operation is top secret. You are to tell no one."

As the three CIA operatives watched the airmen walk away, one said, "So what are we going to do?"

"Go to Alamo and find that cowboy."

"But Sir—we can't just start searching houses. Not without causing a stir."

"Of course not." Using his cigarette as a pointer, the CIA officer said, "You, and you—take the car and go on into town. Just hang around and keep your eyes open. Move around as much as you can without attracting attention. Watch the highway out of town."

"Can we clean up first, Sir?"

"There's no time. He could be gone already. We'll relieve you in the morning." The CIA man tossed the cigarette aside to smolder into nothingness in the dust of the lakebed, retrieved his rumpled suit jacket and hoofed it toward his quarters.

A little over an hour later, the dusty sedan pulled into the dark streets of Alamo. After a slow circuit through the streets of the residential area, the intelligence agents pulled off the side of Broadway and parked nose-out facing the street, where they could keep an eye on downtown and the highway.

A little more than two miles away as the crow flies, Rawhide Robinson sat on a sofa, staring in wonder at the glowing screen of a television set.

Chapter Sixteen

The rattle of the hasp as the key opened the padlock stirred Karen from her somnolence. She sat up and rubbed her eyes as the door opened, then squinted when light from the hallway illuminated her face.

"Get up," Carlo Carlucci growled in his best imitation of a tough-guy voice. "Time to eat."

Karen asked and was allowed to visit the bathroom. She splashed water on her face and dried it with the peeled-up tail of her blouse rather than use one of Carlo's towels. There was no dining table in the apartment. Spuds and Eddie sat on stools at a breakfast bar that separated the living room from the kitchen.

A cardboard box sat on the counter, with wrapped sandwiches and bags of potato chips inside. The gangsters were already at work on the meal, washing it down with canned soda pop. Karen grabbed a sandwich and retreated to the interrogation chair and tucked her feet under herself as she sat.

Carlo settled onto a stool beside his muscle and unwrapped a sandwich, tore open a bag of chips, and popped the pull tab off a soft drink can. Within minutes, the counter in front of him was bare, save a few bread crumbs and the drink can's ring pull. He dabbed at the corners of his mouth with a paper napkin and said, "So, Karen—how's things in Alamo?"

Karen's jaw froze mid-chew as she searched her mind for an answer. Lacking a reasonable response, she resumed chewing and was finally able to swallow the wad filling her suddenly dry mouth. She turned to Carlo and said, "Alamo?"

"Yeah, Alamo. You know—where you live. On Frehner Road."

All she could do was stare at her captor.

"C'mon, Karen—you think I'm stupid? We found your car in the supermarket parking lot. Got your address off the registration tag on the visor. Found some stuff in the jockey box, too. Workin' at Silver State Savings Bank, huh? That'll come in handy."

Again, the blank look.

"Karen, Karen, Karen—you don't think the boss is gonna forget that five grand your deadbeat husband owes just because he's dead, do you?"

The crude wordplay prompted laughter from Eddie and Spuds.

"Well, he ain't. The boss wants his money, and bein' as you was married to that flyboy, the debt's yours. I hope it ain't the only thing he left you."

Karen swallowed hard. "It is. There's no way I can pay you. We're barely getting by as it is."

Carlo smiled. "Yeah, but, you work in a bank, remember?"

It was Karen's turn to laugh. "Like that matters. I'm a clerk. I don't clear 'five grand' in a year."

Carlo kept smiling. "Yeah. So what? The boss figures if you work in a bank, you know where they keep the money."

The implication made Karen's hackles rise. "You think I'll help you rob the bank? You're a bigger idiot than I thought. Tell your boss the same goes for him."

Carlo's smile faded. "Be careful what you say, little lady. The boss don't go in much for disrespect. For that matter, I don't either. Finish your dinner."

Karen stared at the sandwich. "I've lost my appetite all of a sudden."

"Fine. We're leaving."

Carlo led the way; Karen found herself sandwiched between him and Spuds and Eddie as they walked to the long, wide, low car parked in a row of dozens of others under a sun shade that did little good in the glare of the low-hanging sun. Carlo shoved Karen into the back seat and Spuds and Eddie slid in on either side. The car bounced slowly into the street and by the time the gangster at the wheel had the air conditioning adjusted to his satisfaction, he wheeled the car into the parking lot of the grocery store where he found Karen.

He stopped in an isolated far corner of the lot, left the car and air conditioner running, hooked his right elbow over the seat back and turned to Karen. "You go on home to Alamo, little lady. And don't forget we know where you live."

"That's it then?"

Carlo laughed. After a moment, Spuds and Eddie joined in, but their support was feeble. "No, girlie, that ain't it. You just get back to your job in that bank up there and mind your Ps and Qs. We'll be in touch. I don't need to tell you, but I'll say it anyway—no cops."

He nodded at Eddie, who climbed out of the car and held the door open for Karen. Desert heat radiated from the asphalt parking lot and engulfed her as she watched the car drive away. Inside the store, she asked for lost and found and the old lady at the service booth rummaged through a packing crate on the floor and plopped three handbags on the counter.

"Any of these yours?"

Karen identified her purse and the lady dipped her chin to examine Karen over the top of her spectacles. "How'd you lose it?"

Karen hesitated. "I was shopping here the other day and—well, I had to leave in a hurry."

The woman nodded. "Got any identification?"

"In the bag," Karen said.

The woman nodded and Karen unclasped the bag and pulled out her wallet, opening it to display her driver's license.

"Good enough," the lady said.

"Thanks," Karen said and turned to walk away.

"Miss?" the lady said, and Karen stopped. "You're lucky someone turned it in instead of stealing it. You should be more careful."

"Yes, Ma'am."

Karen followed her headlights out of town to the junction of Highway 93 and turned north for home, so keyed up she did not think she even blinked her eyes for the duration of the drive. Turning off the highway onto Broadway and into Alamo, she noticed a dark sedan parked facing the road. The silhouettes of two men inside caused a shiver until she realized it was unlikely the mob would be here already. But the presence of the lurkers was still unnerving—not the kind of thing one expected to see in a small town.

For their part, the men in the sedan eyed Karen's car closely, but settled back into boredom upon seeing the face of a woman at the wheel and no sign of passengers.

"Eric?" she yelled as she opened the kitchen door and flipped on the light. "Eric!"

The ruckus awakened Rawhide Robinson and he sat up on the sofa and, out of habit, pulled on his boots. He rubbed his face with the palms of his hands as consciousness returned, and decided to sit and see what happened next.

He heard the boy's bedroom door crash open and Eric run into the kitchen.

"Mom!" he yelled, his voice still gravelly from sleep. "Mom!"

The yelling stopped, replaced by muffled sobs and the cowboy imagined mother and son locked in a happy hug. After a minute, Eric barraged his mother with questions.

"Are you okay, Mom?

"Where you been?

"Are you hurt?

"What happened?

"Mom!"

Karen laughed and held her son at arm's length. "Eric! I'm fine! Slow down."

Overcome with curiosity, Rawhide Robinson put on his thirteen-gallon hat, crossed the living room, and stopped in the entryway to the kitchen. The woman and boy, locked in a tight embrace, did not notice him at first, then Karen sensed his presence. The sight of a strange cowboy in her kitchen took her aback and she tried for a moment to form words.

Then, “Who are you?”

Chapter Seventeen

The CIA man drove past the agents parked on Broadway, stopped and backed up, swinging his sedan next to theirs, nose out facing the street. He checked the sight lines, satisfied that his subordinates had chosen well—Alamo's business district, such as it was, was visible, as was highway 93, skirting the edge of town. While fresh from a good night's sleep in his quarters at Area 51—officially a detachment of California's Edwards Air Force Base Air Force Flight Center, but located within the Nevada Test and Training Range—he felt dirty from the film of desert dust that seemed to cover him every time he stepped out of doors. He disliked his assignment, but given the ultra-top-secret nature of the work at Area 51, the Central Intelligence Agency maintained a constant presence there. For now, that presence was under his direction.

Stepping out of his car, the CIA man smoothed the front of his suit jacket, already rumpled, like his slacks, from the bumpy drive to town. He climbed into the back seat of the other sedan. The bleary-eyed, sagging faces of the two agents in the front seat watched him.

He fished the cigarette pack out of his shirt pocket, shook out a smoke and lit up. Snapping shut the lid of his silver Zippo, he said, “Well, gentleman, did you see anything suspicious? Anything that might suggest the presence of our wayward cowhand in this burg?”

The agent in the driver’s seat yawned. “Not a thing,” he said, smacking his lips. “Not much traffic on the highway. Everybody in town was asleep.” He yawned again. “Except us.”

“There was one car came into town in the wee hours,” the other agent said. “But it was a woman.”

“Alone?”

“Yessir. Besides, if that cowboy’s around, he’d be going out of town, not coming in, wouldn’t he?”

The CIA man nodded, drew a deep drag on his cigarette and filled the car with exhaled smoke. “Go on back to the base. Get some rest, then file a report. Have it on my desk by end of day.”

“Yessir,” the men said in chorus. They started the car and, when the boss slammed the door, drove away as the sun peeked over the hills east of town. If they hurried, breakfast might still be on at the mess hall. The CIA man watched them drive away then settled in behind the wheel of his sedan, hoping for an appearance by the mysterious—maybe crazy—cowboy. Like a ticking clock, the relentless click, click, click of the button on a cheap government-issue ballpoint pen measured the passing of time.

Hours later, when police chief Lamar Argyle drove past on his way to the Harris house, the CIA man still sat there, sucking on a cigarette and clicking his pen. Not long ago, the lawman had taken a call from Karen Harris.

"Mister Argyle? It's Karen Harris."

"Yes, Miz Argyle?"

"Eric tells me he called you. He was worried when I didn't get home as scheduled."

"Yes."

"Well, I, uh, I—I just wanted to let you know I made it home. So you wouldn't worry, you know."

"Thank you, Miz Harris. Is everything okay?"

"Yes. Yes. I'm fine."

The chief tapped his toe, and listened to his caller breathe. "You sure everything's all right?"

"Yes. Of course. I'm fine."

"Maybe I ought to drive on over and check. Eric was pretty upset. Said it wasn't like you to be late. Insisted there must be something wrong."

"I'm sure that won't be necessary. Really."

"See you in a few minutes, Miz Harris," Argyle said and hung up the phone.

The small house Karen Harris rented had a front door. But, like most homes in Alamo, it saw little use. When visitors arrived, it was the kitchen door, on the side of the house, upon which they rapped their knuckles. When the lady of the house answered Argyle's knock, the heady smell of fresh coffee greeted him along with her nervous smile.

Rawhide Robinson sat at the kitchen table, cradling a mug in his hands. Eric sat beside him, spooning up cereal with determination. Without being asked, Karen poured a mug of coffee for the policeman and set it on the table next to her half-full mug.

"Sit, please," she said. "I guess you've met Mister Robinson."

The cowboy held up a hand. "Please—Rawhide."

"Miz Harris. Eric. Rawhide," Argyle said as he sat.

Eric continued the attack on his cereal bowl as the three adults exchanged glances. Rawhide Robinson broke the silence. "To what do we owe the pleasure, Sheriff? Or is it Marshal?"

"Either way. I've been called worse. Karen called me. She didn't want me to come, but I thought I ought to."

The cowboy's forehead wrinkled, wondering how and when that might have happened. Then he remembered the black box with the little wheel on the wall, and stared at it, still not comprehending the magic it held. *There ain't end to surprises with the boxes they got around here*, he thought. *Telephones, refrigerators, televisions, automobiles….*

"Really, I'm all right," Karen said.

The policeman studied her, wondering at her discomfort. "You look fine—no obvious damage, leastways. But somethin' ain't right."

Karen sipped her coffee, watching the sheriff over the rim of her mug.

"Eric got pretty upset when I mentioned your husban—late husband's—troubles. I guess I spoke out of turn." The woman looked surprised. Shocked, even.

Pausing for a swallow of coffee, Argyle let the revelation sink in. "See, Miz Harris, I was informed by the police in Las Vegas at the time of your husband's passing—Dwight, I believe his name was—that he was in deep with the casinos. Suggested I might keep an eye on you. Didn't seem necessary." He sipped again from his mug. "Until now."

Karen hung her head. When she looked up, she wiped a tear from her cheek, then another from the opposite side. "I'm sorry, Mister Argyle, for your trouble."

"Ain't no trouble for me. It appears you might be the one with the trouble."

When what seemed like minutes passed, Rawhide Robinson cleared his throat. “Ma’am—I think you ought to tell him.”

She snapped a look at the cowboy. “They said no police.”

“’Course they did. That don’t mean you have to listen. Somebody’s got to help you out of this jackpot you’re in.”

“Wish I’d never told you,” she said, struggling now to keep up with the tears. Rawhide Robinson watched with awe as she walked to the cupboard and ripped a square of paper off a roll slick and clean. She used the paper towel to mop her eyes and cheeks then blew her nose.

“He’s right, you know,” the police chief said. “I ain’t much on my own, but I know where to turn for help if needed. I believe we can protect you.”

With a shake of her head, Karen laughed. “Eric, son, why don’t you go outside for a while.” She glanced at the policeman. “Maybe take a ride on your motorcycle.”

Eric looked at Argyle and, seeing a barely perceptible nod, dashed out the door. Within seconds, he kick-started the 90-cc engine of the motorbike to life and peeled out of the yard and onto the dirt track along the irrigation canal and into the desert beyond the house.

“So you know about Dwight’s IOUs,” Karen said.

"Yes. The police down there said the mobsters he owes will stop at nothing to get their money."

Karen swallowed hard. "When Dwight got deployed to Vietnam, he told me to move—said if I holed up somewhere they probably wouldn't track me down. Then when he got killed…. Anyway, he was probably right. They haven't found us—or even tried, so far as I know—since we came here."

"But now?"

"It was a fluke. I was grocery shopping and happened to run into a guy named Carlo Carlucci. He's the one who used to come around harassing Dwight all the time, so he recognized me. Carlucci isn't the boss, but I don't know who he works for."

Over emptied and refilled coffee mugs, Karen told the story of being held captive in the gangster's apartment, and how Carlucci found and rifled her car in the grocery store parking lot to learn where she lived.

"He found a pay stub from the bank, so he knows where I work. Said his boss was happy that I worked in a bank. I'm not sure what they think a clerk at Silver State Savings Bank can do for them, but I got the impression they've got something in mind, or they're planning something."

Pulling a toothpick from the ribbon hatband on his Stetson hat, the policeman gnawed on it as Karen talked.

"Those mafia guys ain't stupid. The more people they got working in banks and the like, the more ways they've got to make illegal stuff look legal. Could be they'll come to you for help laundering money, maybe strong-arm you into embezzling. Could be planning a robbery, even—who knows?"

All this talk may as well have been in Chinese for all it meant to Rawhide Robinson. He seldom had enough money at one time to require the regular services of a bank, nor did the criminal activities described bear any resemblance to the Wild West of his experience.

"I'll talk to my friend down with the Las Vegas police. See what he knows about this Carlucci; find out who he works for and what you might be up against.'

Karen looked skeptical. "What if Carlo finds out?"

"It ain't likely. Just go on about your business like everything's normal. I'll let you know what I learn."

On the way back, he noticed the sedan still backed up facing Broadway. Military and government workers from Area 51 seldom came to town, so the man's presence piqued his curiosity. He turned off the street and pulled in next to the car, stopping with his window only a foot or so away from the driver's-side window of the sedan. Winding down his window, he sat staring at the man smoking inside the sedan. After a bit, the man rolled his window down.

"How's it going?" the police chief said.

The CIA man in the car nodded once.

"Anything you need?"

The man shook his head once.

"Lose something?"

The man again shook his head one time in the negative.

"Good. Thought maybe one of them little green men from Mars you folks keep out there got away or something."

The man said nothing. He stubbed out his cigarette on the window ledge of his sedan and flipped the butt over the top of Argyle's car where it bounced off the emergency flasher's red bubble. Then he rolled up his window.

Chapter Eighteen

Wind-tousled and dusty, Eric rode back into the yard and stood the motorbike on its kickstand behind the house. He came through the door to an empty kitchen. Passing through to the living room, he found Rawhide Robinson sitting on the sofa absorbed in a television soap opera.

"Why are you watching that crap?"

Rawhide Robinson snapped out of his trance and noticed the boy. "It's the only thing on this television set this time of day. Oh, there are different things when you turn that dial, but they're all the same—men going after other men's wives and women going after men that belong to someone else. Heavens to Betsy, it makes a body wonder what the world's come to. Then there's all them little dramas that come along every now and then. Where I come from, womenfolk didn't worry so much about soap to wash dishes and duds and such. Leastways not that I ever knew of—not that I've got all that much know-how when it comes to women."

"You don't have to watch, y'know."

"Oh, I know it," the cowboy said with a smile. "But crazy as these folks on this box are, a man gets mighty interested in what's going to happen next. Besides, staring at this 'TV' you got ain't a whole lot different than staring at the south end of a northbound steer, which is what I've spent a whole lot of my time doing."

Eric laughed.

"Speaking of cattle, there sure ain't many of them on this television on them evening programs. Them boys that's supposed to be cowboys spend all their time drinkin' and gambling in saloons or running their horses all over creation shootin' guns all the time. Don't know how they can rightly be called cowboys if they don't tend no cows."

When Rawhide Robinson finished his rant, Eric said, "Where's Mom?"

The TV aficionado gestured toward the rear of the house. "Back there somewhere. After that lawman left she said she was goin' to get cleaned up and go to town."

"Not Las Vegas! She didn't mean Vegas, did she?"

"Didn't say."

Just then Karen walked into the room, head cocked as she attempted to poke an earring into her earlobe.

"Get washed up, Eric. I'm taking you gentlemen into town for lunch. I left the groceries in the supermarket aisle, so there's nothing in the house to eat except cold cereal and peanut butter and jelly sandwiches. I imagine you two are filled up to your ears with those."

"Great!" Eric said, and hustled off to the washroom.

The modern bathroom held many fascinations for Rawhide Robinson, but he kept his interest in the facilities to himself, out of consideration for the modesty of others.

"Ma'am, are you sure it's safe to be goin' out and about, what with them no-accounts after you?"

"Thank you for your concern, Mister Robinson—"

"—Rawhide."

"—Rawhide. But I don't think they'll be after me yet. Besides, I have to be back at work at the bank tomorrow, and Eric can't miss any more school, so this might be the only opportunity to treat you boys to lunch."

Rawhide Robinson slid into the back seat of Karen's car for the ride uptown. As the car turned onto Broadway, the CIA man in the sedan parked nose-out to the street noticed the silhouette of a thirteen-gallon hat go by. He started the motor and pulled onto the street and when Karen parked in front of the Wagon Wheel café, he slowed and pulled off as well, leaving a distance that would allow him to make certain his recognition of the man in the hat without arousing suspicion.

Rawhide Robinson slipped his hands into his hind pockets and stood inside the door giving the hash house the once-over. It smelled much the same as most eating houses in his experience. But with its big windows and electric lights, the room was much lighter, and all kinds of unfamiliar gadgets stood at attention along the shelves and cabinets behind the eating counter.

They sat and studied menus, the cowboy taken aback at the variety of food on offer, and flummoxed at the unfamiliarity of most all of it. In the end, when Eric ordered something called a cheeseburger, Rawhide Robinson said, “I’ll have the same.” While they waited, Rawhide Robinson asked Eric what he liked to do.

“Oh, just mess around, y’know. Some of my friends have motorcycles, too, and we like to ride out in the desert. We sleep out nights. Sometimes we go fishing down to the Upper Pahranaget. Do you like to fish, Rawhide?”

“Nah, I ain’t never been much for sittin’ around waiting for a fish to decide to get caught.” He tipped his thirteen-gallon hat back and kneaded his chin as if to milk out a thought. “There was this one time, though….”

When he could no longer stand the silence, Eric said, “C’mon!”

“Take your ease, Eric. I’m cogitating on it to make sure I remember it right.”

He thought.

He sipped his coffee.

He thought.

And when Eric started tapping the tabletop with the tines of his fork, Rawhide Robinson considered the tension sufficient and launched his tale.

"It was up in the mountains they call the Sierra Nevada. You-all know where that is?"

Both members of his audience nodded in the affirmative.

"Well, it was late summer and I'd delivered a herd of beef steers over to Sacramento from a spread called Hot Springs Ranch I was a-workin' on up in the Carson Valley. There wasn't no hurry to get back—long as I was there to help with the fall roundup. So I was just takin' it slow and easy across the mountains, watchin' my horse get fat and slick munchin' on that green grass in them high meadows.

"I found myself pretty high up in the mountains, where the slopes was near as straight-up steep as the pine trees. After a day or two, the meadows and the good grazing for my horse was behind us, and we hadn't come across no streams to quench our thirst. The corn dodgers and hardtack in my greasy sack were all ate up, and I was tired of gnawing on jerky. So I set my sights on finding water, thinkin' not only to wet our whistles—which was so dry they didn't whistle no more—and maybe snag a fish to eat. Knowin' how much snow piled up in them mountains of a winter, and with snow still on the peaks up above, I figured there had to be lakes or ponds or pools somewhere, or maybe creeks or streams or rills or rivulets—"

"C'mon, Rawhide!"

"Eric!" Karen said. "Let the man tell his story." The look she cast at the cowboy told him she, too, would like him to get to the point.

Rawhide Robinson also looked to the gathering of other diners affixed on the tale, some going so far as to pull their chairs nearby. They, too, urged him on with their eyes. "Anyhow," the cowboy continued, "there we was, me and my horse easing our way around the face of a cliff on a trail fit only for a mountain goat. On the left was a rock wall as steep and sheer as can be, easing off downward to the right, the cliff face had just enough angle that some scrawny trees and shrub could take root in the cracks and crevices and nooks and crannies in the rock. We come around a turn and, lo and behold, there was a lake right in front of us. Water so clear you couldn't hardly tell it was there at all."

Stopping to sip his coffee, Rawhide Robinson, experienced raconteur that he was, waited and waited for the response he knew would eventually come.

"So what!?" Eric said, loud enough to attract the attention of the few restaurant patrons not absorbed in the story.

The cowboy again paused while his lips visited the rim of his coffee mug. Then, "Well, here's the thing. Other than being made of water, that lake didn't look like any pond I've ever seen."

Another hesitation.

"Get on with it!" an unidentified farmer at an adjacent table encouraged.

"Tell it!" an elderly lady in a floppy hat festooned with fake flowers implored.

"C'mon!" Eric urged.

Rawhide Robinson tipped back his thirteen-gallon hat. "That lake, you see, it didn't spread out before us—it spread up and down."

Stunned silence ensued, soon followed by guffaws, snorts, hoots, howls, and other expressions of disbelief.

"I swear it," the cowboy chronicler said. "That lake was up and down instead of sideways. It wasn't a big lake, more like a pond, really. I'd guess maybe as tall as a *Californio's reata* is long, and near about that distance off to either side. Went down the mountain a distance as well, although I don't recollect how far. There being no breeze to speak of, there was nary a ripple on the surface of that water. It was as smooth as that glass window over there with the "OPEN" sign stuck in it.

"That horse I was ridin' was skittish, as you might imagine. Seein' water standing up like that seemed as strange to him as it did to me. But, after a bit of snorting and snuffling and shuffling around on that narrow little ledge, he stuck his snout out there and sucked in a little of that water. 'Fore you know it, he was muzzle deep in that water, like drinking out of a vertical lake was old hat.

"Me, I dismounted and slithered my way around that horse's shoulder and stepped up to the surface of that lake. I poked and I prodded, I touched and I tapped, felt and fondled, nudged and knuckled that water. Thing was, it acted just like you'd expect water to—it splashed and sprinkled, bubbled and burbled, ebbed and flowed like normal.

"Finally, I decided to dive in. Don't know why I took such a fool notion, as that ain't like me. But, I pulled off my boots and hung my hat on the saddle horn. Then it come to me—there weren't no way to dive into a lake that's standing in front of you instead of underneath you. So I sucked in a big ol' breath of air and walked right in."

Another chorus of disbelief from the assembled crowd assailed Rawhide Robinson, but he sipped his coffee and continued.

"Once under the water—if 'under' is an acceptable term in the circumstances—things was every bit as odd as you'd expect. I could see the bottom in front of me, that water being clear as a summer morning. And there was fish swimming around—well, not around, exactly, more like up and down. They'd paddle past me goin' up and glide by me goin' down. They didn't seem to pay any attention to me—I reckon they'd never seen a human-type animal before. About the time my air was used up, I just reached out and grabbed one of them finny fellers and stepped back out of that pond. Of course, the water was runnin' off me in sheets and streams—but instead of fallin' to my feet, it fell off me sidewards, and splashed right back into that little lake.

"That's all she wrote, folks—all except me and that horse made our way to a patch of lower, level ground and I built me a campfire and skewered that fish and enjoyed me a meal of somethin' besides beef jerky and fresh air. When me and that horse left out of there, we went by a different trail and I made it over the mountains and back to the Hot Springs Ranch in plenty of time to resume my duties in the autumn gather."

As his listeners sat aghast at Rawhide Robinson's story, outside the café the CIA man in the rumpled suit ground out a cigarette with the sole of his wing-tip shoe and stepped into a phone booth. He closed the door, dialed the operator, deposited a handful of coins in the slot, and dictated a report to a subordinate in an office several stories below the dry bed of Groom Lake.

Chapter Nineteen

By the time the CIA man made it back to the buildings at Groom Lake, a meeting was already underway in an underground conference room. Besides the normally unflappable military man who oversaw Area 51 operations, the psychiatrist who released Rawhide Robinson was on hand. Also in the room were the physicists who earlier offered an explanation for the cowboy's appearance, the officer commanding the Air Force Police stationed at Groom Lake, and a liaison from the private contractor that provided many of the support services required by the top-secret operations at Area 51.

The CIA man snapped open his lighter and put the flame to a fresh smoke as the elevator doors closed and had consumed half the cigarette by the time they opened again on the subterranean level hosting the cowboy conference. His footsteps echoed down the long corridor, reflecting off seemingly endless pale green walls. Flinging the designated door open, he passed through the anteroom without acknowledging the Air Policeman standing guard and opened the conference room door.

The psychiatrist was holding forth. "...no danger. The man is off his rocker at best. Seriously delusional, out of touch with his surroundings, and limited in his ability to communicate effectively. As I have said before, any information he conveys to the outside world concerning what he may have seen here will not be taken seriously. No one will listen to him."

"That's where you're wrong," the CIA man said, stubbing out his cigarette butt in an ashtray on the table. He pulled out a chair which screeched across the tile floor and sat. "I saw him in the café in Alamo. The man had an audience around him and they appeared to be hanging on his every word."

"Have you any idea what he was saying?" the military man said.

"No, Sir."

The psychiatrist laughed. "For all you know, he was spinning some windy about his adventures in the Wild West!"

The CIA man's glare bored into the psychiatrist like the death rays rumor had it were being tested at Area 51. "There's nothing funny about this situation, Doctor. The fact that we don't know what the cowboy knows or is saying is a serious problem. We don't know what he is telling people—what secrets he may be disclosing."

The psychiatrist shrugged.

The military man questioned in turn the private contractor and the head of the security police. The doctor sat bemused at their contributions. The CIA man smoked cigarette after cigarette and clicked the button on a ballpoint pen again and again and again. Opinions varied, but the consensus was to err on the side of caution and capture and detain the cowboy.

Discussion turned to how best to seize Rawhide Robinson. A show of force, recommended by the Air Force Security Police commander, gained little support. With many of Alamo's citizens and the broader public already suspicious of and apprehensive about Area 51 and what went on there, a military-style operation to snatch a single, seemingly harmless cowboy was likely to contribute to concerns about operations.

The CIA man suggested a covert operation. Along with a small crew of operatives, he would surveil the Harris home and grab the absquatulated cowhand at first opportunity.

Amused by the whole notion, the psychiatrist said, "And what, may I ask, do you intend to do with him once you've caught him?"

No one proffered a proposal, proposition, or plan; offered a scheme, suggestion, or solution; accorded advice, guidance, or idea; offered a notion, opinion, or recommendation.

The physicists, heretofore uninterested in the conversation, had sat hunched over notepads scribbling signs and symbols, and erasing and whispering, perked up and spoke up to fill the silence. The elder scientist held up a pointed finger, cleared his throat, and said, "Gentlemen, we have some thoughts on that."

*****

The Organized Crime Task Force at the Las Vegas Police Department occupied a dim basement room in an outdated, outmoded auxiliary building well away from the action. One might be led to believe, and many were, that the city's commitment to rooting out the mob was a low priority.

Some saw this as a result of systemic corruption, trickling down from the highest offices in city government to the lowest levels of law enforcement. Had Nevada imposed a state income tax on its citizens, withholdings for graft—if such could be collected—may well have outpaced those from salaries and wages for many in the department. Critics of a cynical nature suggested the very existence of the Task Force was to serve as an early warning alarm for the Mafia should the feds, in the form of the FBI, IRS, DOJ, DOC, ATF, or other abuses of the alphabet start nosing around.

While the depth of mob influence in city government may be arguable, few would deny the existence of widespread leaks in the police department. Nothing else could explain the fact that raid after raid, warrant after warrant, sting operation after sting operation turned up nothing.

And so it is no surprise that within minutes of a call from Lamar Argyle, Chief of Police in Alamo, Nevada, to a friend in the Las Vegas Police Department, an outgoing call from an unnamed member of the Organized Crime Task Force reached an unnamed executive at a certain casino on the windblown, dusty reaches of Las Vegas Boulevard, known in popular parlance as "The Strip."

Within minutes, the telephone rang in Carlo Carlucci's apartment.

The call caught Carlo napping, sleeping off a submarine sandwich, potato chips, chocolate doughnut, and six pack of cheap beer. He lurched upright on the sofa, grabbed his head with both hands, and flopped back down. When the ringing refused to quit, he sat up again, belched with the force of a mountain howitzer, and staggered to the phone on the kitchen wall.

"Yeah, yeah. What is it?"

. . .

"Sorry, Boss—didn't know it was you."

. . .

He covered the mouthpiece on the phone and rolled forth another impressive emission of odiferous aftereffects of erstwhile comestibles.

"Yeah, Boss, I'm still here."

…

"Yeah, I'm listening."

…

"She did? #&%^@! I told that broad no police!"

…

"Yeah. I'll take care of it."

…

"Don't worry! I said I'd take care of it!"

Chapter Twenty

Word about the windy-winding waddy got around Alamo as quick as a chicken chasing a grasshopper. Some of the daytime coffee-shop loafers became barstool dawdlers when the sun went down, and they rendered reports to saloon seatmates. Always on the lookout for fresh entertainment, the socializers at the local watering hole discussed tendering an invitation to the yarn spinner to join them, bend an elbow, and engage in conversation.

Before you could say Rawhide Robinson, a pickup truck pulled away from the Boot Hill Bar, packed in both cab and box bed with convivial celebrants setting out for the Harris household intent on convincing one particularly peculiar cowboy to come back with them for a night on the town. Seldom one to refuse a social occasion, and out of patience with the program offerings on the television set, Rawhide Robinson climbed aboard the pickup truck, occupying the seat of honor his newfound friends and neighbors referred to as "riding shotgun."

Never had Rawhide Robinson seen, or even imagined, the dance of darkness and light in the Boot Hill

Bar. Generally hazy and dim, the interior also sparkled and shined with bright and glowing points of light. Sharp colors, flashes and flickers, even ropes of light in vibrant hues bent and twisted to form words and pictures. The cowboy's eyes locked on one light fixture in particular: the shape of a bottle appeared to pour light into a fancy glass while bubbles drifted out of the glass and into the air.

As the cowboy stood transfixed by the spangled splendor of the neon lights, the Boot Hill regulars dragged several of the bar's small tables together, placed chairs all around, and seated the guest of honor at the head of the makeshift table.

"What can we get you to drink, Mister Rawhide Robinson?" someone said.

"Oh, I ain't much of a drinker—a beer now and then's about it."

"Well, we got plenty of cold beer. What's your pleasure?"

The cowboy pursed his lips, cocked an eye, and furrowed his brow in consideration. Then, "Come to think of it, I'll pass on the brew. I believe I'd like one of those," he said, pointing to the neon light that held his fascination like a leg-hold trap.

"Champagne?"

"I reckon so. I've had a glass a time or two, and that there picture calls to mind how them little bubbles will tickle a feller's nose."

Soon, a glass of champagne sat on the table in front of the captivated cowboy. Given that through the evening he would use his mouth mostly for talking, the beverage would never reach the bottom of the fancy glass.

"Tell us about yourself, Rawhide," a patron requested. "We don't see many strangers around here."

The cowboy sipped at his champagne and smiled as he wrinkled his nose. "There ain't much to tell. Spent most all my time since I was a button punchin' cattle one way or another. Trail drives, roundups, ranches, line camps, ridin' herd—you get the picture."

"Whereabouts you from?"

"Here and there. Raised up in Texas. Spent time most everywhere 'round the West. Froze to death one time in North Dakota, died of heat stroke in Arizona, drowned in the ocean off California, trompled to death in a stampede in Colorado, killed by a wolverine in Wyoming, bucked off a bronc and busted my neck in Nebraska, washed away in a flash flood in Utah—you know, just the usual sorst of things cowboys do."

The ranahan's résumé incited amusement around the table. Then, another question: "What part of the country you like the best?"

Rawhide Robinson considered the question. "Oh, you know, long as there's grass enough for a cow to make a cud, every place has its charms. Thing I've noticed most is how the country's changed."

"How's that?"

"More and more people moving in—more towns all the time, and them that's already there growin' like a sucking calf." He paused and scrunched his nose after another bit of the bubbly. "Strangest thing, though, is when the land itself changes."

The row of wrinkled foreheads around the table, reminiscent of plowed furrows, communicated confusion to the cowboy conversationalist. "You mean like earthquakes and such?" someone wondered.

"That'll do it all right," Rawhide Robinson said. "Floods will make a difference, too. Even the wind…." The bronc buster's banter trailed off and his mind drifted elsewhere. With glazed-over eyes, he seemed to be in another time, another place—at least in his mind.

Rattling bottles and clinking glasses failed to fill the silence to the satisfaction of the assembled listeners. One, sitting near the cowboy, nudged his shoulder. "You all right, Rawhide?"

With a shake of the head, the cowboy came to himself. "Sorry, boys. Seem to have wandered off." He smiled and reset his thirteen-gallon hat. “Now, where was I?”

“You was startin’ to say something ’bout the wind somewhere.”

“That’s right,” Rawhide Robinson said. A sparkle as bright as the Boot Hill Bar’s neon lights illuminated his eyes as he embarked upon his narrative. “It was back when I was ridin’ for a ranch in southwestern Wyoming. Big outfit, it was, mother cows scattered for miles across the country. A long day’s ride wouldn’t even get you to the edge of the range their cattle grazed. You boys ever been to Wyoming? They got lots of antelope there—why, let me tell you about them critters—”

“—What about the wind?” some impatient listener interjected. “You was gonna tell us about the wind.”

The cowboy held up a hand. “Sorry, boys. Sometimes I tend to wander off the trail. The wind. I’m here to tell you, boys, the wind does blow in Wyoming. Spring, summer, fall, winter—it don’t ever quit. Fact is, they say the snow there in winter never melts. It just blows around and blows around till it’s wore out. But never mind that.

“One time I was ridin’ after cattle on the far reaches of that ranch when a north wind came up. Started out gusty and blustery, then settled into a steady blow that kept gettin’ stronger and stronger. Got so the horse I was aboard couldn't buck it no more, and I had to squeeze the apple myself just to keep from getting' blowed out of the saddle. Got so bad we dropped off into the lee side of a dry wash and hunkered down under an outcrop of rock. Even under shelter, that wind like to have peeled a man's hide right off."

Some of the listeners around the table nodded in agreement, having experienced similar streams of air, Nevada being no stranger to a stiff breeze.

"Of course, that wind was stirring up a goodly amount of dust. But as my horse and me squatted there squinting our eyes, dust and dirt and pebbles and stones started into some serious swirling. Then rocks and boulders lifted off and set off southward—some rolling along, others airborne, sure as I'm born."

"Aw, c'mon cowboy—ain't no wind that strong."

"He's right!" another onlooker said. "Dust, sure, even sand. But no way would a wind blow big rocks around!"

"Hold on there! It's Rawhide's story, so let him tell it!"

"Aw, *&#@&^! It can't be so."

Rawhide Robinson raised his hands, stopping the dissent like Moses staving off the Amalekites. "Now, boys," he said. "I know it sounds farfetched. But that ain't nothin' to what happened next."

He stopped for another sip of champagne, sniffing at the stimulating bubbles. He savored the sensation until the crowd grew restless, then he re-launched his tale.

"Remember I said how it felt like that wind would peel off a man's hide? Well, it didn't, but only 'cause I was sheltered under that outcrop. But it did peel the skin right off the earth. Tore a tear in the topsoil and lifted a layer aloft. That layer looked like somebody shaking a rug, the way it floated and flapped."

Rawhide Robinson raised a hand, reducing another rash of incredulity, and continued.

"I swear it's so, boys. Sure as I'm sitting here. Then that wind picked up, if you can imagine such a thing is possible, and started rolling up that layer of mother earth like spooling up a bedroll. It just kept rolling and rumbling along, raising a racket like you wouldn't believe—of course you wouldn't believe it; I wouldn't believe it if I hadn't seen it with my own two eyes and heard it with my own two ears.

"It got dark as night with all that dust, and then it got dark as night on account of it was night. That rumbling and roaring kept up through the night, but it was ever so slowly fading away, off toward the south. Then, just before dawn it quit, the dust settled, and the stars was a-shining in the sky like nothing had happened.

"When the sun came up, I snugged up the cinches on my saddle, climbed aboard that horse, and rode to the top of a low hill there to have a look around. I'll tell you, boys, what I saw was so shocking I couldn't catch my breath."

At that, Rawhide Robinson paused to once again stimulate his proboscis with the fizz of the champagne.

"Well, what did you see!?"

"What was it?"

"What happened?

"Tell it!"

Rawhide Robinson smiled. "All in good time, boys," he said as he took another sip of champagne and smacked his lips with satisfaction. "What happened was, that layer the wind tore loose from Mother Earth had kept on rolling up and winding up and didn't stop till it got to Utah. Turned into a whole new mountain range, it did, and you can see it yet today. The Uinta Mountains, they call it—runs east and west right along the border between that notch in Utah and Wyoming."

"Oh, pshaw!" some skeptic said. "That can't be so!"

Rawhide Robinson laughed. "But it's true, boys! Surely you-all have heard of the Uinta Mountains. How do you think they got there?"

"Well, sure, but—well—that can't be how it happened."

Rawhide Robinson smiled. "Sure it is. I seen it. Besides, why do you suppose them Uinta Mountains run east and west—knowin' that most every other mountain range in the country runs north and south—if they wasn't rolled up by a north wind?"

No one in the audience had an answer. But, to a man, they searched their minds, their memories, their knowledge, their educations seeking an alternative explanation.

And Rawhide Robinson sipped his champagne with a smile, even though the passage of time as he told his tale had somewhat weakened the ecstatic sensation of the tiny bubbles.

Chapter Twenty-One

After cogitating and ruminating on Rawhide Robinson's tale for a time, talk and laughter among the Boot Hill Bar regulars returned to normal. The tale teller himself, still spellbound by the neon signs and other glittering lights in the cozy establishment, looked beyond the glitz to see deeper into the décor.

As is the case with many eating and drinking establishments around the West, burned-in cattle brands from local and far-flung ranches decorated the wooden walls of the Boot Hill Bar. Rawhide Robinson, with long experience deciphering brands, read his way around the room. He stopped, wide-eyed, upon spotting a charred "51."

"Say boys," he said, capturing the attention of the room at large, pointing in the direction of the 51. "That brand there, that's for the 51 Ranch, ain't it?"

"Sure 'nough," said a bowlegged old buckaroo familiar from experience with the annals of cattle ranching in the neighborhood. Then, with a curious glance at the palavering puncher, said, "How's it you know 'bout the ol' 51?"

"Oh I heard tell of it in my travels," he said. "Knew a hand who worked there at one time. Run by a man name of Elizondo, ain't it?"

"It was," the old man said. "The 51's long gone."

Rawhide Robinson let that rest while he removed his thirteen-gallon hat and raked his fingers through his hair. Resetting the hat, he said, "What happened?"

"Ol' Elizondo—Dominique, he was, went by Dom—run the place for years, startin' way back. He died, ol' Dom did, not long after the turn of the century. Hadn't any sons, but a girl of his, Rachel, she kept the place goin' for years. Did a fine job of it, too, she did. Some waddies didn't cotton to ridin' for no woman, but Rachel knowed her business and treated ever'one square.

"Can't say the same for that no-account boy of hers. Bruce wasn't much interested in the cow business. Fool kid never knowed which end of a cow gets up first. Place kinda went to pot with him runnin' it. When them government folks showed up back in the fifties payin' off and runnin' out ranchers to build that base they got out there at Groom Lake, Brucie couldn't cash the check fast enough. Don't know what became of him. Don't much care."

The cowboy considered the account, waiting for the old man to drain off his beer glass before probing further. "What is it they do out there?" he said, not realizing he had seen more of what went on out at Area 51 than anyone else in the room.

With a throaty laugh, the old man addressed the room. "Ol' Rawhide here, he wants to know what the government's up to out there at Area 51!"

The initial reaction was a round of raucous hilarity. Then, answers, elucidations, opinions, ideas, explanations, claims, comments, remarks, and reports came fast and furious—prefaced by the old man.

"Thing is, son, nobody knows what goes on, and there ain't nobody tellin'. It's all hush-hush. We don't hardly ever see anyone from out there and when we do they don't say nothin'. 'Course, that don't stop folks from talkin'."

Which they did.

One claimed a flying saucer—a term wholly unfamiliar to Rawhide Robinson, but he did not interrupt—that crashed in the New Mexico desert in 1947 was at Area 51, where scientists endlessly studied the wreckage, trying to figure out how the thing worked.

Another stated that other scientists were examining the bodies of the space men killed in the crash.

Still another swore some of the space aliens had survived, and were kept at Area 51 for study.

Another claimed there were other aliens and alien spacecraft on the base, and that the visiting space men and government were in cahoots to bring about any number of nefarious plans and programs.

Yet another bore witness that experiments were underway to cross-breed human beings with the space men—or women.

One man believed leaders and employees of the military-industrial complex (another phrase that gave the cowboy pause) had succeeded in developing flying saucers of their own, and swore you could see them flying around at night.

Some postulated the eggheads out there were building jet airplanes (again, a term causing confusion for the cowboy) that were invisible.

Others supposed death rays were under development that could kill over long distances, and against which there was no defense.

One speculated about a vast underground network at Area 51, levels and levels of subterranean chambers to conceal even further the nefarious nature of activities out there.

Another ranted about high-speed underground railways that connected Area 51 with other, similar, top-secret operations across the reaches of the continent.

Someone expounded on experiments in time travel and teleportation.

There were even allegations of attempts to control the weather.

One particularly strident expositor supported his claims with a challenge: "You think they ain't hidin' somethin' out there? Well, friend, just wander out that way and see what happens. Soon as you set foot on the wrong side of the Area 51 fence, you'll be surrounded by soldiers pointing rifles at you."

Rawhide Robinson reeled from the reports. It was overwhelming, astounding, staggering, stunning, mind-boggling, and breathtaking. He had no way to understand, let alone evaluate, much of what was said. At times, it seemed the men spoke a foreign language.

But, beneath it all was one irrefutable truth: The 51 Ranch was gone. He wondered if there was any way to get it back—or, get himself out of this strange time and place and back to work atop a horse.

"Well boys," he said, "It has been an enjoyable evening. Can't remember when last I enjoyed such convivial company. But, my eyelids keep slammin' shut so I wonder if someone of you-all would haul me back to the Harris place so's I can engage in some serious slumber."

Chapter Twenty-Two

The long, wide, low, heavy automobile gobbled up the miles and left them in its wake, an hour or so still to go before reaching Alamo. For about the five-hundredth time, Carlo Carlucci fiddled with the knobs and vents on the car's air conditioning system as he piloted the ship. Eddie occupied the other front seat. Spuds sprawled across the big bench of the back seat, snoring and snorting as he slept the sleep of the innocent—or, in his case, the unindicted.

Eddie yawned, said, "What we gonna do when we get there, Carlo?"

The mobster adjusted one of the vents streaming cold air, held up a hand to ascertain the precise direction of the flow, and altered the outlet a minuscule amount.

"When I talked to the boss yesterday, I told him we'd take care of it. So that's what we'll do—take care of it."

"Yeah, sure—but how we gonna take care of it?"

"I don't know yet. We'll think of something."

The silence returned for another mile or two, then Eddie said, "Why'd she go and call the cops, anyway?"

"Beats me. She'll learn better by the time I'm through with her."

"Why'd we have to leave so early?"

Carlo looked at his sidekick as if he had just asked the stupidest question in the history of organized crime.

Eddie persisted.

"So we'll get there by morning! What do you think?" Carlo said.

"But why?"

Carlo thought for another mile, then shrugged. "I don't know. Seemed like a good idea at the time."

Another mile passed. Carlo said, "You got any ideas what to do?"

"I dunno," Eddie said. "I guess we could snatch the woman again."

"I already thought of that. But she can't get us no money if we got her under wraps. Besides, the boss wants her goin' to work at that bank. He thinks that could come in handy."

"So why don't we just leave her alone?"

"Don't be dumb, Eddie. She went to the cops! We gotta do something!"

Spuds snorted in the back seat, then said, "Snatch the kid."

"What!?" the occupants of the front seat said in unison.

"Snatch the kid. She's got a kid, don't she?"

Carlo thought for half a mile. "Yeah. Yeah she does. Spuds, you're a genius."

The big man in the big back seat was not aware of the compliment, as he had resumed snoring and snorting. For his part, Carlo continued steering the ship, now with a smile on his face and a plan bubbling away in his brain.

*****

The approach of the automobile from Las Vegas along Highway 93 toward Alamo mirrored the course of a smaller, darker, nondescript sedan traveling the gravel road from the back gate of Area 51. At the wheel was the CIA man. Beside him rode one of his most trustworthy operatives; another nodded off in the back seat.

The CIA man fingered a silver Zippo lighter out of his shirt pocket and touched the flame to the cigarette dangling from his lips, then exhaled a stream of smoke into the already vaporous interior of the sedan. "Wake up!" he said. "No sleeping on duty!"

The man in the back seat jerked his head upright, looked around bleary-eyed and attempted to stifle a yawn. He scrubbed his face with the palms of his hands, then turned to watch the rabbit brush and yucca and Joshua trees stream by in the halo of the headlights.

"Sir, what's the plan when we arrive in Alamo?" the front-seat passenger said.

The driver checked the rearview mirror to see that the agent in the back seat was still awake. "We have ascertained that the culprit has taken shelter at the home of one Karen Harris, employed as a clerk at Silver State Savings Bank. Also residing in the home is her minor child, a fourteen-year-old boy who attends the local school.

"The abode in question lies at the end of a residential street, parallel but not connected to the highway. It is somewhat isolated from neighboring domiciles, which should simplify our mission. We will locate a site near the residence from which we can set up surveillance without drawing undue attention to ourselves. Once the female occupant vacates the premises and proceeds to her place of employment, and the boy leaves for school, we will approach the dwelling and apprehend the cowboy."

The CIA man checked the mirror to ascertain the wakefulness of the back seat agent, then glanced at the agent beside him. "Understood?" Both men answered in the affirmative.

"There are two points of egress from the habitation. Each of you will be stationed near one of the doors to prevent escape should the malefactor attempt to flee. The road into the residence essentially ends there. A dirt track continues for some distance along a canal bank but is not passable for a passenger car and offers no concealment for an offender fleeing afoot. I do not anticipate difficulty if you execute the plan as outlined. It is absolutely essential that we capture the cowboy with a minimum of disquiet. Stealth is vital. Understood?"

Again, the agents answered in the affirmative. The one in the backseat yawned. "But suppose he tries to escape? Are we authorized to light him up?"

"Only as a last resort. Discharging our weapons would attract attention, which we wish to avoid." The CIA man smiled a sort of sneer, or a leer, or perhaps a smirk. "But if he does attempt to effect an escape…."

The sedan rolled slowly through the streets of Alamo in the dim light of early dawn and made its way to Frehner Road. As the car neared the Harris residence, the CIA man extinguished the headlights and rolled on in the dark, then backed the car off the road and parked between a hay rake and baler in a cluster of farm implements. "Stay awake and alert," he said to his agents as he marked time with repeated clicks of a ballpoint pen.

Inside the house, Karen Harris slathered jam on a slice of toast and rushed through a cup of coffee. She made sure Eric was up and around, getting ready for school. On a normal day, she ushered him out the door long before leaving for work at the bank. But, recent circumstances being what they were, she had fallen behind in her work and intended to get caught up before the doors opened to the public. Not that the Silver State Savings Bank was prone to crowds of customers, but much of her work as a clerk was time-consuming and tedious, and she hoped to start the business day fresh.

When she came out of the house, the CIA men sat up straight in their seats. The agents watched as she started her car and drove toward town, raising a cloud of dust as she went past.

"Apparently the woman doesn't keep bankers' hours," the operative in the back seat said.

The CIA man nodded. "All the better for us. Gets her out of the way early."

A while later, the door opened again and Eric came out carrying a handful of schoolbooks.

"Be on the alert, men. Our man's on his own in there now. We'll let the boy get out of the way and then we'll move in."

"You're sure he's in there?" said the man in the back seat, checking the magazine on his government-issue Remington M1911A1 semi-automatic pistol.

"Sure as can be. We know he has been staying at the house, but there has been no recent surveillance. We will proceed on the assumption that the culprit is inside."

As they watched Eric walk away from the house, a car the size of a battleship roared past, stirring up enough dust to obscure the house and everything else in the vicinity.

"What the—!?" the CIA man said, flinging open the door to stand next to the car, pistol in both hands and resting atop the roof, aimed in the general direction of the house.

Enough of the dust settled to allow the agents to watch the big car pass Eric, then wheel around in a skid.

Inside the car, Carlo Carlucci yelled, "That's him! That's the kid—I seen a picture of him in the woman's car! Grab him!"

Before Spuds could summon sufficient wakefulness to allow action, Eddie was out and around the car. He grabbed a startled Eric by the scruff of the neck, jerked open the back door and shoved him onto the seat next to Spuds, slammed the door, reversed his route, and climbed back in next to Carlo.

"Step on it!" he said.

Carlo did.

Rousing by the ruckus, Rawhide Robinson stepped out the kitchen door bareheaded, in sock feet, and with a mug of coffee in hand in time to see Eric shoved into the car. He, along with the entranced CIA agents, watched the big automobile speed back up the street. In less than a minute, it roared past again, this time going south on Highway 93, visible in spurts between clumps of trees. The cowboy tossed the coffee into the dirt and hurried back into the house, only to emerge again in full cowboy regalia—sans chaps and spurs, which remained folded and stacked near the end of the sofa upon which he slept.

Although he could not explain why, Rawhide Robinson knew the men who nabbed Eric were the same men who had held Karen captive. He wished he had paid more attention to the operation of the telephone so he could call the local lawman. Lacking any alternative, he would go after him in person. Urged by the need for speed, he thought to tame the boy's motorbike and ride it into town. His time as a passenger, watching Eric control the beast, offered a basic idea of the machine's operation.

"There he is!" one of the intelligence agents hollered as Rawhide Robinson pushed the bike off its kickstand, turned the key and kicked the starter pedal. He revved the throttle and released the clutch lever and the motorbike lurched forward and died. The cowboy kicked the starter and tried again, this time jerking and jolting along until the cycle's speed caught up with the too-high gear the amateur rider had inadvertently chosen by stepping too often on the gearshift pedal.

With boot heels bouncing and dragging in the dust, the cowboy tried to control the motorbike, which seemed driven by a mind of its own. The cycle weaved and wobbled, careened and canted, ducked and dived like a salty bronc. The discombobulated cowboy looked up in time to see the CIA sedan pull onto the road and stop, blocking his way to town. When the door opened and the CIA man in the rumpled suit stepped out and leveled what must have been a pistol of some kind at him, Rawhide Robinson cranked the handlebars, urging the motorcycle to change direction, accomplishing a U-turn.

He twisted the throttle and sped past the house and onto the trail along the canal. He nearly lost his seat as the motorbike lurched forward when he popped the clutch after stomping his way to a higher gear and more speed. He chanced a backward glance and saw the CIA car coming on fast. He stomped on the gear shift again and twisted the throttle and tried to keep the cycle on the rutted, rocky, and ever-narrowing path along the ditch. Looking back again, he watched the car stop and the agents scramble out and point their pistols at him. He ducked low over the handlebars and twisted the handle-grip throttle even harder, thankful he heard no shots over the whine of the engine.

Once the imminent danger seemed past, the cowboy concentrated on the finer points of motorcycle procedure, fiddling with the hand and foot controls, becoming familiar with their interplay.

The irrigation ditch he rode beside paralleled the highway, and when a culvert offered an opportunity to cross, he did so, using a potholed access road to a hay-field to get to the highway. He crammed his thirteen-gallon hat tight on his head and urged more speed from the motorcycle as he followed Highway 93 toward Las Vegas.

Somewhere up ahead, on the same highway, was the big car carrying Eric and his kidnappers.

Chapter Twenty-Three

The White River is an occasional stream that starts and stops and starts and stops and goes across miles and miles of Nevada desert. In the Pahranagat Valley, fed by water from Crystal Springs and Ash Springs, the water-course creates a narrow strip of green that allows for the very existence of Alamo.

Rawhide Robinson, astraddle Eric Harris's Honda motorbike, followed the verdant ribbon for a dozen or so miles south from the town, at which point the stream spread out to form Upper Pahranagat Lake, then again at Lower Pahranagat Lake, after which the water more or less got lost in the desert. At that point, the dry river's streambed—sometimes called Pahranagat Wash—coursed through a Mojave Desert serious about its business, painting the landscape near and far every shade of dun the cowboy had ever seen on a horse's hide, with some additional hues thrown in for good measure.

As he rode, eating up miles at a rate the cowboy could not believe, it came to him that he had no idea where he was going or what he would do when he got there. Oh, he understood in a general sense that he was on the way to Las Vegas to rescue Eric from the clutches of the Mafioso malefactors who had snatched him from the street. Beyond that, the details were a bit dim. So dim, in fact, he could not see them at all.

He realized he needed help. He did not know how or where he was going to get it. Then he saw the first sign of civilization since leaving Alamo some forty miles ago. A ways off the highway huddled a cluster of tin buildings—long and thin and reminiscent of railroad cars, but lacking any semblance of strength or substance. Turning onto the short access road, he read a sign on a pole as tall as the mast on a sailing ship: *Betty's Coyote Springs Ranch*.

Tires skidded in the gravel when he stopped to study the place. It did not look like any ranch he had ever seen. No corrals or cattle pens, no barns or outbuildings, no horses, no cattle. *Oh, well. It ain't the strangest thing I've seen since gettin' caught out in the rain*. He urged the motorbike forward and stood it on its kickstand near a doorway under a sign similar to the one on the pole, and climbed the steps. He raised a fist to knock, but saw a paper stuck to the door reading "C'mon In, Pardner!" So he did.

He found himself in a dim room furnished with a pair of overstuffed sofas and matching chairs, and a short bar with a few stools cuddled up next to it. A portly woman with painted eyes sat behind the bar on a stool, icy drink in hand and cigarette smoldering in an ashtray.

"Welcome, cowboy. Can I get you something to drink? Or would you rather I introduce you to the girls?"

The nature of the ranch dawned on Rawhide Robinson. His face reddened and he found himself at a loss for words. But speechlessness is a condition that never held the cowboy in its grip for any length of time, and he swallowed hard and managed to mouth, "No, thank you, Ma'am. I come lookin' for some help."

The woman looked around the empty room. "As you can see, we're not exactly overwhelmed with activity just now, so I suppose you can tell me your sad tale."

So he did. He had worked it out in his mind that the only course of action that made sense was to call Alamo chief of police Lamar Argyle—if only he knew how to work one of those telephone gadgets. Somehow, the woman spun the little wheel on the black box and talked to someone, then someone else, then, "Lamar? Is that you, honey? It's Betty." She exchanged pleasantries with the lawman for a bit, then said she had a man who wanted to talk to him.

The cowboy held the phone against his face as he had seen others do, but nothing happened.

"Say hello, or howdy, or something," the woman whispered.

"Hello?"

"Rawhide? Rawhide Robinson? That you?"

The cowboy almost dropped the phone, surprised and shocked and startled by the policeman's voice, sounding for all the world like he was in the same room. He gathered his wits and explained the situation. Argyle allowed he would be there as soon as he could get there, and advised the cowboy to sit tight.

"You sure you don't want something to drink?" the lady said after hanging up the phone. "It'll take Lamar the better part of an hour to get here."

He requested a tall glass of water, climbed onto a barstool, and settled in for the wait. Before long, the residents of the ranch wandered into what passed for the lobby and took their seats on the sofa and chairs, curious about the visitor. Unable to resist an assembled audience, Rawhide Robinson struck up a stream of conversation with the scantily clad ladies.

Soon running out of small talk and convivial chit chat, conversation turned to travel.

"What brings you to Nevada?" one of the ladies said.

"Oh, you know," the cowboy said. "I just kind of drifted into this country, and took up a job punchin' cattle." He took a sip of water, contemplating how to continue the tale. "But that job—well, it sort of disappeared on me. Right now, I guess you could say I'm between jobs. Could be ridin' the grub line before long."

"Where were you before?"

"Been about everyplace you can imagine—everywhere they run cattle, that is. Babysitting bovines is most of what I've done. This sure is a hard country for raising cattle you folks have got here."

In answer to further questioning, he opined—meaning no offense, of course—that there were plenty of better places to graze mother cows and raise fat calves. "Down in Texas, we got miles and miles of grass, growin' thick as a parson's beard. Good grazing in places in California, too—Oregon, Idaho. Best place is probably them Great Plains—Oklahoma, Colorado, the Dakotas, Kansas, Nebraska. I'll tell you ladies, I ain't never seen a place that'll grow grass—and darn near anything else you plant—like Nebraska will. Let me tell you about this one time…."

He paused to sip his water and let the tension build, as accomplished story tellers are wont to do. Sensing the anxiety was at a fever pitch, he set his story afloat.

"Years ago, long years ago, I was trailin' a herd of cattle through Nebraska on the way to Miles City, Montana. We come across a crew building a railroad—leastways they wanted to build a railroad. Seems they hadn't done a very good job layin' in supplies, 'cause they had miles of roadbed built and miles of steel rails to lay track, but they'd run plumb out of railroad ties and spikes.

"So, there they was, pulled up short on the Nebraska plains with nothin' for all them workers—gandy dancers, bridge hogs, jerrys, muckers, snipes, and such—to do but spit and whittle and play poker. Well, them railroad bosses was fit to be tied, as it would take weeks for a shipment of ties and spikes to arrive.

"There was this old Nebraska sodbuster hangin' around and he took the feller in charge of construction aside for a private conversation. After they palavered a while, the railroad man sent a man into the supply tent and he came out totin' a keg of shingle nails and loaded it onto that nester's wagon. Then he pulled up next to the mess tent and loaded up a carton of toothpicks. And he drove off."

Another interlude ensued as Rawhide Robinson traded his glass of water for a cup of hot coffee. The girls held off as long as they could, but patience wore thin.

"Is that it?"

"What kind of story is that supposed to be? It don't mean nothin'."

"Don't this story have an end?"

The raconteur ranahan sipped the foam off his cup and encouraged the ladies to hold their horses, so to speak, while he quenched his thirst. Then, "Here's what happened. A couple of days later—two days most likely, but it could have been three—I don't remember precisely—that plow-chaser came back with a loaded wagon. Following him was a whole string of farm wagons. Must've recruited every sodbuster in all of Nebraska to help him haul that freight. Took the better part of a day for them railroad workers to empty all them wagons of railroad ties and steel spikes. Had enough to lay another eighty-nine miles of track, if memory serves."

"Where'd they come from?"

"How'd that farmer get that stuff?"

"How'd he do it?"

Rawhide Robinson smiled. "Like I told you, ladies—the soil in Nebraska is so fertile farmers can raise any kind of crop. What that nester did was sow his fields with them toothpicks and shingle nails, and durn near overnight they growed into cross ties and railroad spikes."

It took a moment of shocked silence for the import of the story to take root. Then the audience verbally assaulted the storyteller, heaping upon him every known iteration and expression of disbelief in the English language, with a few foreign phrases thrown in for good measure.

But the aspersions soon turned into a tempest of tee-hees and twitters, giggles and guffaws, chortles and chuckles the likes of which had never before been heard nor seen—neither in terms of quality nor quantity—at Betty's Coyote Springs Ranch.

Chapter Twenty-Four

Holstering their pistols, the CIA agents watched the quarry race away, leaving a rooster tail of dust behind the screaming motorbike. The man in the rumpled suit banged his fist on the roof of the sedan and released a string of epithets not found in any government manual guiding decorum.

"Load up! We can catch him if we hurry—let's go!"

"Sorry, Sir," said the agent who vacated the passenger seat. "We won't be going anywhere."

"What?"

"Flat tire."

Stomping around the car, the CIA man eyed the deflating tire and listened to the hiss, singing harmony with the ticking of the cooling engine. "#%@&!" he said, repeating some of his earlier obscenities and adding a few more for good measure. Backtracking to the driver's door with even more vehemence, he jerked the keys from the ignition and, following a few unsuccessful efforts to stab the key into the lock, opened the trunk. "Get it changed." He ripped off his suit jacket and tossed it into the car and paced, clicking ballpoint pen in hand, as his subordinates wrestled with hubcap, tire iron, lug nuts, and bumper jack.

"What happened back there?" the operative balancing the spare tire asked. "Who were those guys in the pimpmobile?"

The man in the wrinkled shirt shrugged. "Wish I knew."

"You think they've got anything to do with our cowboy?"

"Don't know. Whoever they are, and for whatever reason they were after that kid, they sure threw a wrench in the works. We would have apprehended our escapee. I don't know if the cowboy knows who they were, or if he's out to rescue the boy on general principle."

The sweaty agent on the end of the tire iron snugged the lug nuts a final time, handed the tool to the other agent and slapped the dust off his hands. "So what do we do now?"

Staring southward, the CIA man mulled the inquiry for a moment. "What's down there?" he said, with a nod down the narrow valley.

Neither agent answered for a time, wondering if it was a trick question of some kind. Finally, one said, "I don't know. Nothing much until you get to Las Vegas."

"Precisely. Based on the car they drove, I'm guessing that's where the men that snatched the kid are going.

And that must be where the cowboy's going. So," the CIA man said, slipping back into his rumpled jacket and lighting a cigarette, "that's where we're going."

An hour later, the sedan roared past Betty's Coyote Springs Ranch on Highway 93 without so much as a glance at the landmark. Had they looked, and had their eyes been sharp, they would have noticed Eric Harris's Honda motorbike parked just outside the front door. The cycle's erstwhile driver, at that very moment, was inside the legal establishment in the desert regaling Betty's ranch hands—for want of a more family-friendly description—with tales of his adventures in the Wild West.

Half an hour or so after the government agents passed the place, lawman Lamar Argyle did see the cycle as he wheeled into the dusty gravel patch that served as a parking lot. He entered the house of ill repute to find Rawhide Robinson holding court before an antechamber chock full of convivial Coyote Springs occupants. Every girl in the place lined up for a buss on the cheek as the cowboy made his way to the door, and many—perhaps most—maybe all—slipped a redeemable souvenir Coyote Springs poker chip into his pocket.

Rawhide Robinson found Karen Harris in the passenger seat of the police car with the red bubble on top. Pale and drawn, and blinking back tears, she sat still as stone. The cowboy climbed into the back seat and reached over to pat her on the shoulder.

Argyle said, “I went by the bank to let Karen know what happened. She wouldn’t let me leave without her. She knows these mobsters, so she’ll likely be good help.”

Karen said nothing, sitting and staring into nothingness.

“Right friendly bunch of ladies Betty’s got there,” the celebrated storyteller told the policeman as they left the ranch and accelerated onto Highway 93.

“Yup. Betty sees that her girls keep their noses clean,” Lamar said, gnawing on a toothpick. “Tell us again what happened this morning, so Karen can get it firsthand.”

Rawhide Robinson related in detail the adventures in Alamo. He told of stepping out into the morning, planning to sit on the step and sip coffee. And about how a big car coming from town disrupted the peace and quiet, circled around quick as a cutting horse, stopping only long enough for one of its occupants to nab Eric, then whizzed away, back the way it came. And how it reappeared on the highway, heading south.

The cowboy related his attempt to borrow the boy’s motor machine and track down the policeman. And how his desires were thwarted when the man in the rumpled suit and his sidekicks blocked his way with their automobile. And how he turned and raced away in the opposite direction, down the track along the ditch with the car hot on his heels. And how the car stopped when the trail got too rough. And how he just kept going, trailing after Eric and the men who absconded with him. And that he soon realized he was on a fool's errand, as he knew nothing about what lay ahead and that, if his experiences of late were any indication, what he encountered would be so bizarre and beyond his understanding that he would be at a loss as to how to aid the boy. And about how he determined to stop for help in reaching the lawman at the first place he came to—never realizing it would be so far away.

"Thank goodness Betty (Rawhide Robinson feeling comfortable in the circumstances addressing her by her given name) was willing to come to the aid of a poor unfortunate cowboy," he said in conclusion.

Lamar tossed the remains of his frayed and frazzled toothpick out the window and replaced it with a fresh one from his hatband. "Did you recognize the man who nabbed Eric?"

"Never seen him before."

"What did the car look like?"

Rawhide Robinson described it as best he could, lacking as he did any of the conventional knowledge and accepted understanding of automobiles or the vocabulary to describe them. It was black, he said, and long, low, and wide with a kind of pointy nose with a shiny, kind of v-shaped doodad on it. And silver—lots of shiny silver, on the front and back and a stripe down the sides.

"That's Carlucci's car, all right," Karen said through her fog.

The policeman said, "How about the other car, Rawhide? Have you ever seen those men before?"

"One of 'em. The feller driving that car, he was one of them I seen out at the place where I lost my horse. Kind of ornery, he is. Nervous-like, too—and he smokes a lot. Asked me all kinds of questions and wasn't any too happy with my answers."

"I believe I know who you mean," the lawman said. "He's been hanging around town—him, or others just like him. They're government agents of some kind." Argyle weighed his next question. "What does the government want with you?"

"Don't know as they do. Could be something to do with that place they got out there."

They rode along in silence for a time, a condition not in keeping with the cowboy's loquacious nature. "This town we're going to—Las Vegas—what's it like?"

"Hard to say," Lamar said. "I can tell you it ain't like anyplace else you've ever been."

"You mean like Betty's ain't like any other ranch I ever seen?"

Lamar laughed. "Yeah, I guess you could say that. Las Vegas is a kind of 'anything goes' kind of place."

"What do folks there do?"

"What do you mean?"

"Well, are they farmers? Miners? Millworkers? They raise cattle? Work in factories? What kind of work do they do?"

Again, the lawman chuckled. "No, nothing like that. See, people from all over come to Las Vegas to have a good time. Mostly to gamble, eat, and drink. Most everyone who lives in the city has some kind of a job or other making sure the tourists have a good time."

"Tourists?"

"Tourists—you know, people on a tour, visitors, people taking a vacation."

"You mean they come here for no particular reason? Just to play around?"

"Yep. That's what Las Vegas is all about."

Rawhide Robinson ruminated on that for a minute or two. He decided it must be a small town if its only reason for being was playing around. After all, who would want to waste time on such tomfoolery?

Chapter Twenty-Five

The Alamo Police car topped the hill and Las Vegas lay before them. It did not look like much in the harsh desert sun. Clumps of high-rise buildings and clusters of businesses stood here and there, with houses sprawling in all directions. Dusty desert stretched beyond toward every point of the compass. Although much larger than Rawhide Robinson had imagined, he saw little in the city to convince him that it amounted to much.

Karen Harris, too, studied the city as they approached. After a few minutes, she said, "I grew up here, you know."

"That right?" Lamar Argyle said.

"Yes. My parents still live here."

"That right?"

"Yes. But you wouldn't know it. I haven't spoken to them in years."

The policeman did not question her. And while Rawhide Robinson's curiosity overflowed the back seat, he said nothing.

After a time, Karen continued. "I met Dwight while I was still in high school. He was stationed at Nellis for flight training. Mom and Dad didn't think much of him—to them, he was just another fly-by-night flyboy. Lots of them are—but I thought Dwight was different. I ended up pregnant. My parents wanted no part of it—all but disowned me. Me and Dwight got married. He was away on maneuvers a lot, but he did his best to provide for us. Then he took up gambling, and things got worse."

Karen sniffled, swallowed, and wiped the corners of her eyes. "Carlo Carlucci started coming around, threatening Dwight."

Lamar cleared his throat. "Did he threaten you?"

"Not really. Not in so many words. But he had a way of asking me to let Dwight know he'd stopped by that left me shaking all over every time. He was always polite—and that was the worst part. He would smile, but you knew he didn't mean it. Dwight was relieved, almost happy, when his unit got called up to go to Vietnam. Last thing he did was tell me to take Eric and get out of town. Out of sight, out of mind, he thought. I thought he was right until I ran into Carlucci at the grocery store."

"So this Carlucci feller's a mean one," Rawhide Robinson said from the back seat.

"He sure acts like it. But it's hard to say how much of it is an act. In a way it's almost funny—like he imagines himself in a gangster movie or something. He never seemed particularly bright, either—like someone else was doing all the thinking for him."

Argyle said, "What about the two men with him?"

Karen smiled. "Eddie and Spuds. Those two are even dumber than Carlo. I don't think they could think for themselves if they had to. I'd say the three of them share one brain, but even at that they don't use all of it." Then, as if the thought had just occurred to her, "They might be dumb—but I don't think any of them would hesitate to shoot someone if they were told to."

An airliner passed overhead on approach to land at the Las Vegas airport. The cowboy ducked at the roar of the jet engines and looked out the side window to watch the plane sink toward the landing strip. "What is that thing!?!"

"Airplane," Lamar said.

"That don't tell me a thing. What is it? What's it for?" Rawhide Robinson noted the similarities—and the differences—between this flying machine and the one he saw at Area 51. While this one was much larger, it seemed less threatening than the other—that one reminded him of a bird of prey, while this one was more like a big, fat goose.

"Remember those tourists I told you about? The ones who come here to play? Well, that's how lots of them get here. They fly in from all over the country—all over the world, for that matter."

The cowboy tipped his hat back, wiped the shine off his forehead, and pressed as close to the window as possible to follow the airliner's descent. "You mean there's people in that thing?"

Lamar looked at Karen. Karen looked at Lamar. They both cranked around in their seats to look at Rawhide Robinson.

The police chief eventually found his voice. "Well…yes. That's what the airlines do—they fly passengers all over the world."

"How many people's in that thing?"

"Don't know for sure—about a hundred-and-fifty, I guess. Maybe more."

"How often does it come?"

"What?"

"How often does one come? Every week or so? Every day?"

Lamar and Karen laughed. Karen said, "I read a while back that there are more than a hundred flights a day into Las Vegas."

"A hundred!" The cowboy screwed his hat down, furrowed his forehead, and started manipulating the fingers of both hands as if tallying a herd of cattle. "Well butter my butt and call me a biscuit!" he said. "That's fifteen thousand people! Where do they put 'em all? What keeps the place from fillin' up and overflowing?"

Seeing that the cowboy's surprise was genuine, Karen and Lamar tried, with limited success, to keep from laughing. Lamar said, "They don't stay long. Only for a week, maybe two. Then they go back home. While they're here, they stay in hotels and motels. Besides, all them airplanes ain't full. Some days, only five thousand people come to town."

Now the cowboy laughed. "Still, there ain't nobody got that many hotels! I been to Chicago, Illinois, and I don't think they got that many."

Karen said, "Probably not. Hotels is about the only thing there is in Las Vegas. There's hundreds of places to stay. Thirteen thousand rooms for rent, according to what I've read."

Rawhide Robinson sat stunned and stupefied. He studied the town as they drove, thinking there must be more to it than the sun-bleached, seedy, shabby, shopworn city that now surrounded him. "What's that thing?" he said, pointing off to the east.

"It'll be a hotel, if they ever get it finished. They've had financial difficulties—lots of starts and stops," Karen said.

"Hotel? Looks more like a giant toadstool."

Lamar laughed. "Supposed to look futuristic—like a space ship or something."

"You mean like they say is out there at that Area 51 place?"

Lamar laughed again. "If you believe the stories."

Rawhide Robinson shook his head. "I don't know what to believe anymore. Whole world's gone plumb loco."

Somewhere else on the streets of Las Vegas, a nondescript government sedan crept along with the traffic. The agent in the back seat rolled his window down and used his hand to waft some of the smoke outside.

"Well, here we are in 'Fabulous Las Vegas,' Boss. Now what?"

The CIA man swept ashes from the lapel of his rumpled suit. "That cowboy's lookin' for that Harris kid. We find the kid, we'll find the cowboy."

"How we gonna do that?"

"Somebody snatched the kid for some reason. Looked like a mob job to me. The FBI's got an office here. Maybe, just maybe, those idiotic G-men can tell us something."

Chapter Twenty-Six

It wasn't until Carlo Carlucci rolled into Las Vegas in his oversized automobile that he wondered what he would do with Eric Harris. Snatching the boy off the street seemed like a good idea at the time, but in hindsight he wondered. He considered stashing the kid at his apartment. Eddie said it would not work.

"Why not?"

"Think about it, Carlo! We locked up his momma at your place—she knows where you live. Once she realizes the kid's gone, where's the first place she'll look?"

Carlucci considered the idea and realized Eddie was probably right. "So what are we gonna do?"

Eddie shrugged.

Spuds snored.

Eric spoke his first words since being apprehended by the gangsters. "You could always take me home, y'know."

Carlo snorted. "What good would that do, kid?"

"What good will it do to keep me?"

"When we turned your ma loose, we told her not to call the cops."

"So?"

"So, she did!"

"What's that got to do with me?"

The mobster had no answer.

"Look," Eric said, "just let me go. I'll call Mom to come and get me. I won't tell the police—honest."

Carlo's face pursed and puckered, wrinkled and creased, furrowed and knitted. His brain did likewise as he deliberated and cogitated, speculated and contemplated. "Nah. That ain't gonna work. How we ever gonna get the money your old man owes us if we let you go?"

"How'll you get it if you don't?"

"I don't know for sure. Your ma will come up with something—if she wants you back, that is."

Eric sighed. "She ain't got no money, y'know."

"Yeah—but she works in a bank. The boss, he's got a few ideas. Until I talk to him, you ain't goin' nowhere."

Spuds stirred. "We gotta go somewheres, Carlo. We can't keep him in the car and drive around all the time."

Eddie said, "I know! We'll take him out to the Stardust and stash him in one of the rooms there. Nobody'll ever find him—heck, they won't even look there."

Carlo considered the idea for a moment, then set a course for the Strip.

Even at midday, the Stardust casino bustled. Bells dinged, buzzers hummed, wheels spun, coins rattled, handles ratcheted, roulette wheels whirled, cards shuffled, dice rolled, lights glowed and glimmered and blinked and winked and flashed. Carlo and Eddie led the way into the chaos, Eric behind, Spuds brought up the rear.

"Keep movin', kid—you ain't allowed in here only to pass through," Carlo said.

Eric ogled the endless rows of slot machines, craps and blackjack tables, and other gambling paraphernalia. Alone, in twos and threes, in groups large and small, people were coming and going from every direction. All except the gamblers, who stood and sat and slouched and slumped as if hypnotized by their game of chance of choice.

Watching and waiting until his handlers were occupied threading their way through a mob of people coming the other way, Eric ducked off into a row of slot machines. He ran down one aisle, turned down another, then turned into another row to double back toward where he started.

He was long gone before the gangsters realized he was missing. In a panic, Carlo sent Spuds and Eddie off in different directions while he made his way to a security door and climbed the stairs to the "eye in the sky" catwalks that spread like unseen spider webs throughout the casino. Eric slipped through the coming-and-going crowds and through a dark doorway into one of the Stardust's lounges. Only a few drinkers patronized the place and no one noticed the boy slide into the corner of a booth in the darkest corner of the room.

Carlo saw no trace of Eric through the one-way glass, and for a few minutes watched Spuds and Eddie thread their way through the ranks of slot machines and the pit in a futile effort to locate their quarry. On Carlo's orders, a radio call from a catwalk supervisor soon had the casino's entire security force on the lookout, searching for a fourteen-year-old boy matching the description Carlucci passed along.

Hunkered low in the booth, Eric waited. His heart raced when a uniformed guard stepped into the lounge. The man's walkie-talkie squawked and hissed as he waited for his eyes to adjust to the shadowy room. After scanning the room—stopping to study each of the customers, but seeming to pass over Eric without notice, he walked out into the casino. Taking a position near the door, he keyed his radio to life. In no time at all, more security guards arrived and stationed themselves at every possible means of escape from the lounge. While the others stood guard and awaited the arrival of

Carlucci, Spuds, and Eddie, the first guard re-entered the lounge.

Thinking himself safe, for now, Eric contemplated his next move. Lost in thought, he did not notice the security guard stop at his table. A flashlight beam stirred him from his wool-gathering.

"Lemme see some ID, kid. I don't think you're old enough to be in here."

His way off the booth bench blocked by the uniform, Eric slid down and shot out from under the table. He scrambled past the guard and reached the doorway, but came up short as it was blocked by the bulk of the man called Spuds. The mob muscle wasn't quick, but he was solid and strong and his grip on the back of Eric's shirt collar was sure. The boy punched and kicked and squirmed and snarled, but his activity came to resemble that of a marionette when Spuds lifted him off the floor and let him dangle at arm's length.

"Give it up, kid. You ain't goin' nowhere," Spuds said.

Eric sagged like a deflating balloon. Spuds lowered him till the boy's feet barely touched the floor and kept a firm grip on his collar as he half shoved, half carried the boy on through the casino. Eddie grabbed the boy's arm for extra security and Carlo stayed close behind. The parade stopped briefly in what served as the hotel lobby while Carlo conferred with a desk clerk and came back with a key. They exited onto an outdoor walkway and near the end of a long row of guest rooms, he unlocked a door and stepped aside to let Spuds and the boy through. Carlo handed Eddie his car keys and told him to bring the car around. He hung the "Do Not Disturb" sign on the doorknob and locked the deadbolt and chain latch.

"Don't even think of trying anything, kiddo." He shoved Eric onto the bed and closed the window curtains. Dragging a chair to the door, he told Spuds to take a seat and block any attempt by Eric to get out the door. Carlo turned on the television and flopped into the room's other chair, picked up a tourist magazine off the table and proceeded to flip through the many and varied attractions of Fabulous Las Vegas.

"What're we gonna do?" Spuds said.

"I dunno. I'll think of something."

When Eddie tapped at the door, Spuds pulled his chair aside and let him in. Eddie tossed the car keys to Carlo and sat on the edge of the bed.

"Move out of the way!" Eric said. "You're blocking the TV."

Eddie looked at the glowing box, looked at Eric, and slid to the other corner of the bed. Carlucci tossed the magazine onto the table, stood and hitched up his pants.

"You two stay here. I'm gonna go find the boss." Spuds repeated his dance with the chair and Carlo undid all the locks. Before closing the door, he said, "Lock it back up and keep an eye on the kid."

Hours later, Spuds awakened to the sound of the key in the lock. He unlocked the dead bolt and slipped the security chain from its latch. Carlo came in, carrying two large pizza boxes and a six-pack of canned soft drinks, all of which he deposited on the table.

"The boss, he's thinking," Carlo said. "Wants us to sit on the kid until he figures out what he wants us to do. Spuds, you're stayin' here tonight. Eddie, come with me."

Last thing before closing the door on his way out, Carlo said, "Spuds—don't even think about getting out of that chair."

Chapter Twenty-Seven

Smoke drifted in the close air of the small office. The CIA man stubbed out his cigarette, fouling the pristine ashtray the FBI agent pushed across the desk. Looking around the room, the CIA man noted similarities to his own workplace—same pale and putrid green paint on the walls, same gray and white tile on the floor, same nondescript metal desk. Even the same government-issue ballpoint pen, he noticed, as he picked it up off the desk and clicked the button.

One of the intelligence operatives sat next to the CIA man in the rumpled suit on an identical metal chair with a thinly padded seat and back. The other agent slouched against the wall in the corner, scraping tire grime from under his fingernails.

"That's it? That's all you've got?" the FBI agent said. The notepad before him on the desk remained clean. Placing his standard-issue government ballpoint pen on the untouched paper, he sat up straight in his chair. "No license plate number? Not even a partial?" The FBI man's suit jacket, shirt, and tie were as crisp as his counterpart's were disheveled.

"That's it. Black. Lots of chrome. About the size of a battleship. I thought you golden-boy G-men with all your magic tricks could track it down."

The FBI agent laughed. "Half the wise guys in Las Vegas drive cars that meet that description. I would have thought CIA spooks could come up with a better description, what with your world-renowned skills at intelligence gathering."

"No need to get smart," the CIA man said, firing up a cigarette. He slipped the silver lighter back into his pocket.

"I'm afraid 'smart' is standard issue at the FBI," the agent said with a smirk.

"Yeah, right. So put some of the smarts to work and help us figure out who kidnapped this kid. You G-men still handle abductions, don't you?"

"Sure. Once it's established a kidnapping has occurred."

The CIA man spat out a lungful of smoke. "We saw it happen. What more do you need?"

"Well, a report from the family—even the local police—would be useful."

Click, click, click went the pen. The CIA man gritted his teeth to bite back annoyance. "The kid's mother was at work. Probably still is. Could be she don't know yet the kid's missing. The 'local police' is one old guy in a Stetson hat. He's probably on a stool at the town choke-and-puke drinking coffee and eating doughnuts."

"Still…."

"Still, nothing! There's gotta be something you can do. The kidnappers are surely gangsters, and this is the Organized Crime and Racketeering Division, ain't it?"

"Well, yes…."

"What about the cops? You got contacts there?"

With a smile, the FBI man said, "We don't liaise with the LVPD. Ask them what time it is and you'll have every mob boss in town checking his watch."

"That bad?"

"That bad. The corruption runs pretty deep."

"So what do we do?"

The FBI agent shrugged. "Why don't you boys run on back to Area 51 and protect those space aliens you keep out there and we'll see what we can find out about this purported abduction. A boy snatched from the streets of Alamo, Nevada, by suspected mobsters driving a nondescript car—nondescript, at least, on the streets of Las Vegas—doesn't give us much to go on." He smiled and shook his head, then fixed his gaze on the CIA man. "And if we see a cowboy on a motorbike, we'll let you know."

The intelligence officer clicked the pen one more time and tossed it onto the desk, stood and mashed the butt of his cigarette into the ashtray, and brushed ashes from his rumpled jacket. “G-men,” he muttered as he walked out the door, followed by his two operatives.

“Spooks,” the FBI agent mumbled as he straightened his tie.

*****

Karen Harris directed police chief Lamar Argyle to the supermarket where she’d been captured and later released by Carlo Carlucci. Driving around and around through neighborhood after neighborhood from there all afternoon, she finally located the apartment complex where the gangster lived. A tour of the parking lot did not reveal his car.

The policemen said, “He’s got to come home sometime, but I don’t see no sense in sitting here waiting for him. Karen—you said Dwight mostly gambled at the Stardust?” With her affirmative answer, he drove away, allowed as how they should get a bite to eat and check out the casino then come back.

Karen said, “Maybe we should go to the police.”

“I sure wouldn’t,” Rawhide Robinson said.

“Why not?”

“Look at it this way. Them bad guys told you not to go to the law, didn’t they?”

"Well, yes. But I did."

"Yeah, but there ain't no way they could've knowed that. They only found out when ol' Marshal Argyle here talked to his policeman friend on the telephone. It didn't take long for those gangsters to come after you after that. So somebody from the police had to've told 'em."

Karen sighed. "I guess you're right. But why Eric and not me?"

"My guess," Argyle said, "is they came after you, but saw Eric and figured it'd be better to grab him. Think about it. Whatever their boss has in mind for you won't happen if you're held hostage."

After supper, the police chief invited the cowboy to sit in the front seat. "There's something I want you to see," he said as they drove off into the twilight.

Rawhide Robinson's eyes widened to the size of fried eggs when the car turned onto Fremont Street. Flashing, streaming, blinking, flickering, running neon in every color imaginable lined the street, covering the buildings and reaching into the sky. Lamar parked the car, and the cowboy stood on the sidewalk, gleaming lights reflecting in his expansive eyeballs.

"I'm seein' it, but I don't believe it….

"I been in prairie fires, but compared to this, they ain't but sputterin' fat candles….

"Would you looky there—a big ol' cowboy wavin' howdy...

"Why, this is prettier than a fat calf on good grass..."

The astounded cow puncher turned round after round on the sidewalk, reading signs and basking in the glow.

"I thought them lights in that Boot Hill Bar in Alamo was somethin' to see. But this—well, it's...it's...it's..."

History will record in its "Annals of the Amazing and Incredible" the night Rawhide Robinson talked himself into a loss for words. He opened his mouth time after time as if to speak, but closed it again and again when words would not come. Despite his rich vocabulary, he could not find suitable exclamations, adjectives, similes, nouns, ekphrases, aphorisms, hyperbole, grandiloquence, metaphors, superlatives, enumeratio, or analogies to give voice to his astonishment.

The world, in the cowboy's eyes, was getting curiouser and curiouser.

Chapter Twenty-Eight

Still spellbound by the light displays at Casino Center on Fremont Street, Rawhide Robinson barely blinked as Lamar drove down The Strip. As they pulled into the Stardust, his eyes sparkled nearly as bright as the roadside sign with its swarm of glittering stars. Then there was the giant spectacle stretching across the building front. He did not know what to make of the giant Earth ball, the cosmic rays, the spinning planets, the galaxy of bursting stars, or the word "Stardust" in enormous letters, repeated on either side of planet Earth.

"You'd recognize Carlucci and his goons if we see one of them inside?"

"You bet, Lamar," Karen said. "I spent too much time staring at their ugly mugs to forget them anytime soon."

"Well, let's go on in and take a look around. There'll be a crowd, so let's take it slow and easy. You see one of them, try to stay out of sight. C'mon," Argyle said, and stepped out of the car. "Rawhide, try to keep your jaws together. Open-mouthed like that, you look like a tourist."

The casino cacophony assaulted the trio as they passed through the entry doors. The time-warped cowboy's eyelids spread and his jaw dropped despite his best efforts to maintain some semblance of composure.

He was no stranger to gambling—most saloons in his experience hosted a poker table or two and a faro layout. Larger establishments at cattle shipping towns often included roulette wheels, craps tables, and a variety of card games. But the gambling parlors in Rawhide Robinson's history, in sum, in total, combined, put together, if joined, if pooled, if aggregated, in full, added together, did not begin to equal the ways of wagering laid out before him—even disregarding the banks and rows of spinning and jangling and flashing slot machines, offering mechanized games of chance of which he knew nothing.

Dragging Rawhide Robinson with them, Lamar and Karen found a wall outside the traffic pattern to lean against and from where she could peruse the crowd, ignoring the customers and concentrating on the casino workers. Every few minutes they would relocate, allowing the nervous mother to study a new section of the gambling resort.

Peering into a dim lounge featuring stage entertainment, Rawhide Robinson reddened to a glow rivaling neon. "Tie a knot in my cinch if them women ain't near as naked as the day they was born!" he said, doing his best not to ogle the dancers on the platform. "If you don't count them feathers, that is."

Lamar laughed. "Welcome to Las Vegas, cowboy."

After circling the casino, the lounges, the restaurants, and hotel lobby without seeing Spuds, Eddie, or Carlo, the sleuths drove back to Carlucci's apartment complex. "There it is! That's it!" Karen said, spotting the mobster's big car in its assigned slot as soon as they entered the parking lot. Leading the group through the network of sidewalks threading through the buildings, Karen located Carlo's apartment. Nothing from the front revealed any life inside, so they rounded the building to the communal patio and swimming pool.

"That one," Karen said, pointing out the sliding glass doors behind which she was held hostage. Dim lights illuminated the interior, but they saw no movement or activity.

"Where'd they keep you in there?" Lamar said.

"Small room at the front. No window. Do you think he's got Eric in there?"

Lamar thought it over. "Could be, but I doubt it. He knows you know about this place. He probably isn't dumb enough to think this wouldn't be the first place we'd look."

"So what do we do?"

“Keep an eye on him. We’ll wait here overnight and see what morning brings. He leaves, we’ll follow him. If we’re lucky, he’ll lead us right to Eric.”

After a trip to the supermarket to stock up on snacks and soft drinks, the threesome hunkered down in the car, parked where they could watch Carlucci’s car in case he decided to leave in the night. It didn’t take long to run out of small talk. Lamar stretched and yawned, then said, “Say, Rawhide. I was told back in Alamo that you told some cockamamie tale in the café about some lake somewhere that runs up and down, instead of being flat.”

Karen laughed. “I can testify to that. I was there.”

“It’s true,” Rawhide Robinson said. “All of it.”

“Whaddya mean ‘all of it’?” Lamar said. “You mean it’s true you told the story?”

“That’s true, all right, but so’s the story. Every word.”

Lamar shook his head. “You expect me to believe that?”

“Don’t much matter to me, one way or t’other. I seen that lake with my own eyes, quenched my parched throat with its water, even ate a fish I caught in that liquid habitat.”

“Hmmmph.”

"Say what you will, Marshal. It's all true. If that horse I was ridin' at the time was here, you could ask him. He'd swear to it."

Karen laughed and Lamar couldn't help joining in. He said, "And how about what you told them hang abouts at the Boot Hill? That true too?"

"Sure is."

"I didn't hear that one," Karen said.

"How did you hear, lawman? You wasn't there. You wasn't at the café, either."

"Alamo's a small town. Ain't much that goes on that I don't hear about one way or another. Besides, I make it my business to know what's goin' on."

Karen said, "So what did he tell them at the bar?"

"Oh, some nonsense about the wind in Wyoming making a mountain range. Ain't that about it, Rawhide?"

"More or less. But it ain't nonsense. You ever been to Wyoming?"

"Can't say that I have."

"You, Karen?"

"Not me."

"That's a darn shame," Rawhide Robinson said. "Had you ever been there, you'd believe me. Wind blows in that place like you ain't never seen. There was this one time I was ridin' for a ranch up there, an outfit over around Medicine Bow, it was. Pretty good grazin' in that country. Calves fatten up right nice. Leastways they would if it wasn't for the wind."

The cowboy paused and pulled the tab from a can of root beer. "This stuff ain't bad. Ain't as good as the sarsaparilla I get back home, but it's right tasty."

"Rawhide!" Lamar said. "What do you mean about the wind keeping the calves from getting fat?"

"I'm gettin' to it. Don't get all het up." He paused for another sip of root beer and reached into a cellophane sack and sampled something called cheese puffs that reminded him of chewing on crunchy air. "Ridin' that range wasn't easy. There was the wind, of course, tryin' to blow you right out of the saddle. But what that eternal and infernal wind did to the cattle in that country made it nigh on impossible to keep track of them."

Again he took a hiatus for refreshment. Again, Arglyle argued for continuation, joined, this time, by a similar plea from Karen.

"Here's the thing. Them cows had to adapt to that wind, otherwise they would have blowed away. So what happened was, they got narrower and narrower, so when they turned tail to the wind they didn't offer any resistance. I swear, them cattle wasn't no more'n an inch wide. Looked plumb normal from the side, but didn't hardly show at all from the front or the back.

"What you had to do, then, if you was to round them up, was ride around and around in circles all the time to even have a chance of seein' them. Wore out a lot of horses trying to herd them critters, I'll tell you."

"Oh, Rawhide!" Karen said.

"*&#@%!" Lamar said.

"Now, hold on—think about it for a minute. With them Wyoming cattle bein' flat like that, there wasn't any other way to find them but to ride around till you got to where the sides of them showed. But that ain't the worst of it."

Another interval.

"Well, what?"

"Tell us!"

Rawhide Robinson licked the root beer foam from his lips and said, "The worst time came in the spring when the cows started dropping calves."

"Why's that?"

Another sip of root beer.

Another cheese puff.

"Why?!"

"You see, if them narrow cows, or their calves, ever was to lay down—like they will—they'd be right flat to the ground, and you couldn't see them at all if the grass was more'n an inch high. Missed a lot of cattle at brandin' time on account of that, we did."

Karen did not know what to say.

Nor could Lamar render a response.

Rawhide Robinson sipped his root beer, reset his thirteen-gallon hat, smiled, scrunched down into the car seat, and settled in for the night.

Chapter Twenty-Nine

Click, click, click went the ballpoint pen as the CIA man rode the elevator into the bowels of Area 51. Down a long hallway, he opened the door he was looking for, passed through the anteroom and into the conference room. He took off his suit jacket—fresh this morning, but, as if by some wicked magic, already rumpled—and hung it on the back of the chair then sat down. Reaching for an empty ashtray in the center of the table, he fished a pack of cigarettes and Zippo lighter from his shirt pocket and fired up a cigarette. The CIA operative exhaled a cloud of smoke that carried across the table and enveloped the psychiatrist seated there. At one end of the table, the two physicists involved in their earlier meetings huddled over note pads, scribbling equations and whispering. The chair at the head of the table sat empty, but was soon filled when the military officer in his crisp uniform entered the room and sat.

"Gentlemen," he said, taking a sheaf of papers from a file folder and tapping the edges on the table. He laid the stack before him and smoothed the top sheet with the palm of his hand. "I am given to understand there have been developments in our pursuit of the intruder."

"It's not good news, I'm afraid," the CIA man said.

"Fill me in, please."

Accompanied by cigarette smoke and the clicking of his pen, Area 51's senior CIA operative told how the cowboy surfaced in Alamo, sheltered by a woman named Karen Harris and her son Eric. For unknown reasons, he said, the cowboy made contact with the town's one-man police force. The agency set up surveillance at the Harris household, intending to apprehend the target once the woman and child vacated the premises.

Unfortunately, just after the Harris boy left the house, apparently to attend school, and the intrusion into the domicile and apprehension of the fugitive was imminent, an unidentified automobile interrupted the mission and the occupants seized the boy and drove away, leaving town on the highway south toward Las Vegas.

Pausing to exchange his stub of a cigarette for a fresh one, the CIA man told how the subject of their search witnessed the kidnapping—if that, in fact, is what it was—and managed to activate a small motorcycle parked behind the house and set off in pursuit. "It was obvious the cowboy didn't know how to drive the thing, but he got it going and started down the road. We blocked his way, but he reversed course and set off into the fields and desert. Our pursuit was interrupted when the rutted dirt track became a rocky cow trail. A flat tire, ruptured by the rough road, ended the chase."

The psychiatrist laughed. "What you're telling us is that a deranged cowboy on a boy's motorbike outsmarted and outmaneuvered the Central Intelligence Agency."

A severe glance from the military man brought a halt to the doctor's amusement.

"Our assumption, based on evidence of the man's attachment to the Harris boy, was that he would attempt a rescue," the CIA man said. "With Las Vegas being the only reasonable destination of the kidnappers, hence the cowboy, we left for there as soon as we got the tire changed, hoping to outdistance our subject with superior speed. We failed in attaining our objective."

The CIA man told of the lack of cooperation from the FBI office in Las Vegas, and how the pretentious agent refused to even acknowledge a kidnapping had occurred or the probable participation of the local Mafia in the abduction. "With more than four hundred hotels and motels with some thirteen thousand rooms—not to mention thousands of private homes and apartments—where the boy could be concealed, without local assistance we did not know where to begin to look. Neither would the cowboy, of course, but ferreting him out from among nearly seventy thousand residents and tens of thousands of visitors was an unreasonable expectation, so we abandoned the chase and returned to the base."

"What do you plan to do now?" the military man said.

The psychiatrist interrupted. "If you had any sense, you'd abandon this fool's errand and forget the whole thing."

"#$@%&*!" the CIA man said. "We will not rest as long as he is on the loose. Sooner or later, we suspect the subject will return to Alamo or surface in Las Vegas. We've since learned that the local Alamo policeman is involved, and he and the boy's mother are now in the city. They will, most likely, involve the Las Vegas Police Department and the FBI. Sooner or later, the cowboy will surface. When he does, we'll hear about it. And when we do, we'll collar him."

Again, the psychiatrist. "Can't you see you're wasting your time? Give it up, for goodness' sake. The man's as loco as they come!"

Expelling a lungful of smoke in the doctor's direction, the CIA man clenched his jaws and said, "Not on your life! The man's a security risk! We know he's already been talking."

"Yes, he has! And you know as well as I do what he's been talking about."

Despite its intensity, the psychiatrist did not flinch under the CIA man's stare.

The military officer raised a hand. "Please, gentlemen. This isn't getting us anywhere. Doctor, apparently you know something about the cowboy's activities."

"Yes, I do. And so does he," he said, pointing at the CIA agent. "At the Wagon Wheel café in Alamo, he held forth at some length about how he once encountered a vertical lake in the Sierra Nevada mountains. Later, at the Boot Hill Bar, he insisted to one and all assembled that the Uinta Mountain range is the result of a windstorm, which he witnessed."

"How do you know this?" the CIA man demanded.

Laughing, the doctor said, "You spooks aren't the only ones who hear things. That crazy cowboy's stories are the talk of the town. The point is, nobody is going to believe anything he says—about what he saw at Area 51, or anything else."

"So you say. It is still essential for security reasons that we apprehend him."

"Oh? And what will you do with him once you've caught him?"

"Find out what he knows!"

Again, the psychiatrist laughed at the CIA man's intensity and, he believed, paranoia. "Then what?"

The CIA man offered no reply. He sat back in his chair staring at the doctor, clicking away with his ballpoint pen.

"Uh, Sir," the senior physicist at the far end of the table said with his hand raised as if waiting to be called on in class.

"Yes?" the military man said.

"As we mentioned before, we believe we might have a solution. But the cowboy must be returned to the base if it is to work."

"And what is it you plan to do?"

"We would rather not say at this juncture, Sir. It is theoretical at this stage—and will be experimental at best. But we have been working on computations and equations and formulae and equivalencies, and the associated mathematics and physics. We believe it offers a reasonable likelihood of success."

The military officer sat silent for several minutes. The only sound in the room was breathing, and the incessant clicking of the CIA man's ballpoint pen.

"It is obvious that divisions remain, gentlemen, and that we are not of similar minds. I am not certain as to our best course of action. I see no harm in continuing as we are, at least for the present. We can determine a more certain course in the future. But, for now, catch the cowboy."

Chapter Thirty

Rawhide Robinson reached over the seat back to shake Lamar Argyle awake. “I think that’s them,” the cowboy said.

Although it was mid-morning, the faces of all three were smeared with sleep, eyes and mouths filmy from fitful attempts at slumber in the confines of the Alamo police car.

The lawman lifted himself to full height in the driver’s seat and reached across to nudge Karen. “That them?” he whispered, for no good reason.

Karen gave her fatigued eyes a knuckle massage and yawned. “Yes. Carlo’s in the leisure suit. That’s Eddie with him.”

Argyle waited until the gangster’s big car was clear of the parking lot before starting the engine and rolling slowly toward the street. “I’d best hang back a ways. The bubble-gum machine on the roof of this car is likely to spook him.”

Karen nodded in agreement. Rawhide Robinson did not bother to ask. Since awakening on a ridge of the Papoose Range above the dry bed of Groom Lake he had grown accustomed to being flummoxed by much of what he saw and heard. The few days that had passed seemed like a lifetime.

From quiet residential streets to larger arterials and to the main highway through town, the policeman followed the big, black car into increasing traffic. "Looks like he's headin' for the Stardust."

Compared to the rosy glow of nighttime lights, Rawhide Robinson found the Las Vegas strip bleak and unimpressive in the harsh light of day. Their former glory dimmed, he saw the resort casinos lining the strip—Sahara, Desert Inn, Thunderbird, Sands, Dunes, Riviera, Hacienda, Silver Slipper, even the Stardust—as no more impressive than the leavings of a herd of cattle along a trail.

The mobster-mobile turned in at the Stardust, but bypassed parking stalls near the front entrance to drive to the rear of the complex, and around the rear of rows of buildings lined with guest rooms. The big car turned into a lane between two of the buildings and into a parking space in front of a door identical to all the others along the row.

Lamar stopped at the end of the lane. Karen watched Carlo as he inserted a key into the knob. He pushed the door, but it held fast. He knocked, and after a bit the door opened a crack, then wide. Carlo and Eddie went in and the door closed. A few minutes later, the door opened again. Spuds came out and headed for the casino.

Karen said, "That's Spuds. Eddie went in with Carlo. You think they've got Eric in there?"

"Wouldn't be surprised," Lamar said. "We'll wait a while and see what happens."

"Well, you men keep an eye on things. I have to find the ladies' room."

"I don't know if that's a good idea. You go into the casino, could be you'll run into Spuds, or one of them other hoodlums."

"Not to worry. I'll go over by the Horseman's Park. They've got restrooms back there."

Rawhide Robinson perked up. "Horseman's Park? You talkin' real horses, or somethin' make believe like most everything else in this here town?"

"Oh, it's real horses, all right. The Stardust built a rodeo arena and stables and other stuff. I'm surprised you didn't smell it."

The cowboy rolled down the window and took a deep breath. "I ain't sure what kind of stink I smell, but it ain't got nothin' to do with horses—or anything else that's alive. Marshal—can you hold down the fort while I mosey along with Miss Harris here and have a look-see at this horse place."

Lamar waved them away and settled in to watch the room.

Karen and the cowboy doubled back beyond the row of buildings and turned down a lane past a parking lot toward the Horseman's Park. The lines of parked cars turned to rows of pickup trucks, then pickup trucks with trailers hitched to the tail. Karen walked on to the building housing the restrooms while Rawhide Robinson lingered to look over the trailers, fascinated with the means of conveying livestock.

He wandered to where several mounted cowboys sat, all eyes on the action in an arena. Stopping by the fence, he watched a narrow gate across the way spring open and a steer run out. Horses on either side followed, cowboys aboard with loops at the ready. One cowboy spun his loop two or three times and cast a long shot, the rope settling over the steer's horns. He turned off, taking his dallies, angling the steer as the other roper threw a loop that snagged the steer's hind legs. As he pulled the slack from his rope, the other rider spun his horse to face the steer, both lariats pulled tight. It was over in mere seconds.

Their actions were familiar to Rawhide Robinson, given his years of experience handling ropes and cattle. But it all happened in a rush, rather than at the deliberate pace of ranch work. Then, to his amazement, the cowboys undid their dallies and released the steer, following it down the arena and through a gate. No tripping or tying the steer, no doctoring, no branding, no work at all.

He watched as the action unfolded with another steer and pair of cowboys, then another. An amplified voice that seemed to come from nowhere and everywhere carried on a lot of nonsensical patter, including announcing the names of the cowboys and time divided into seconds and tenths of seconds.

Overcome by curiosity, Rawhide Robinson approached one of the watching cowboys. "Pardon me, son. I wonder if you'd tell me what's goin' on here."

The young rider looked at him as if he had just asked the dumbest question in the history of the world. Any cowboy—even one in old-fashioned dress and an oversized hat—ought to know what was happening in the arena. "Team roping," he said.

"Team roping? But what for? Them boys is just catching them cattle and turning them loose. Why?"

The cowboy laughed. "You're kidding, right?"

Rawhide Robinson tipped back his thirteen-gallon hat and shook his head. The blank look on the cowboy's face convinced his interlocutor of his sincerity.

"It's just a contest. A jackpot. Every team ponies up an entry fee to compete. We all rope ten head, and the fastest combined time wins the jackpot—well, most of it. The fastest time in each go-round wins some, and second, third, and fourth place in the average gets paid, too."

Under questioning, the cowboy explained some of the finer points of team roping rules—the barrier to give the steer a head start, penalties for beating the barrier or catching only one hind leg, disqualifications and such. "You rope any?"

Rawhide Robinson laughed. "Not like this. I've worked cattle all my life, even been in a ropin' contest or two—but nothin' like this. You boys is pretty handy with them ropes. I'm obliged for the information."

Aware all of a sudden of the length of his absence, Rawhide Robinson tipped his hat to his newfound friend and headed back to the car and Lamar—and, by that time, most likely Karen—and the stakeout. He hadn't gotten far when he saw Eric running through the parking lot with Eddie hard on his heels. Catching up fast was Carlo in his big car. Lamar tailed Carlo, the red light on his police car flashing and siren blaring.

Eric, glancing back to see Carlucci's car coming, ducked off between the parked cars, dodging from one to another and dashing across rows to stay ahead of Eddie. Carlo skidded to a halt at the barrier at the end of a row and the police car boxed him in. The gangster bailed out of his car to join Eddie in the chase, but Lamar was faster and stopped the gangster at the point of his gun. Karen cut through the parked cars to follow Eddie and Eric. Breaking out of the parking lot, the boy and his pursuer kicked up dust and they ran through a vacant lot of undeveloped desert.

"Son! I need the borrow of your horse!" Rawhide Robinson said, gasping from the run back to the cowboy he'd been talking with. He pointed to the pursuit through the empty field. "That kid's got real trouble!"

The roper swung out of the saddle and Rawhide Robinson found the stirrup as soon as it emptied, hoisting his leg over the cantle even as he tugged the rein, turning the horse toward his objective. Threading his way through the trucks and trailers, he broke out into the dusty desert lot at a high lope. He picked up the coiled rope hanging from the saddle horn and shook out a loop. The rope was stiffer than what he was used to, but the feel of a lariat in his hands was familiar.

Angling to intercept the race, he fell in behind Eddie. The well-trained horse kept pace, positioning the roper at a comfortable throwing distance. Rawhide Robinson spun the loop overhead a time or two to gain momentum then threw a heel shot that would have made the competitors at the arena proud—and did, as they were all watching. As he reeled in the slack in his rope with a jerk and took his wraps around the saddle horn, the horse, without encouragement, slid to a stop.

Before he knew what hit him, Eddie's nose plowed a furrow in the desert dirt. Keeping the rope taut, Rawhide Robinson dismounted, patting the horse's neck in appreciation. Ignoring the gangster's tirade of obscenities, he stood over Eddie, bent his captive's knees, jerked his arms behind his back and tied them there, rendering him helpless.

From the arena, a cheer arose.

The cowboy remounted, tipped his hat to the impromptu audience, and rode to where Eric stood, slumped over with hands on knees, struggling for breath. "Climb aboard boy," he said, extending a hand and freeing the left stirrup for Eric. Eric settled in behind the cantle and the pair rode back to the arena.

Lowering the boy to the ground, Rawhide Robinson dismounted, flipped the reins over the horse's head and handed them to the owner. "Thanks, pardner. That's a right fine horse you've got there."

"No problem," the cowboy said. "You were pretty handy roping and tying that man. Wanna enter the jackpot?"

Rawhide Robinson laughed. "Thanks just the same, but no. You boys rope and dally faster than I can think. I'm afraid I'll have to pass." He extended a hand and thanked the cowboy again. "I'll fetch your rope back to you once we get it off that no-account."

Weaving their way through the trucks and trailers on the way to the parked cars, the cowboy questioned the boy as to his well-being. Eric was no worse for the wear. In fact, he said, laying around a motel room watching TV, eating pizza, and drinking soda pop wasn't a bad way to spend some time. But, he confessed, the company could have been better.

Karen wrapped her son in a teary hug from which, despite his best efforts, he could not break free. Face florid from embarrassment, he ducked his head and endured. With the boy safe, Rawhide Robinson went to fetch Eddie.

Stardust security guards had converged on the scene by then and milled around. Carlo Carlucci sat in the open door of the Alamo police car, head bowed over cuffed hands. Lamar Argyle fended off questions and commands from the security guards, bouncing from one heated discussion—perhaps better described as vociferous arguments—to another. Despite their demands and protestations, he refused to turn over Carlo Carlucci.

"We'll see 'bout that," one of the security goons said. "Our boss is on the way."

Chapter Thirty-One

Uniformed Stardust security guards gathered round the Alamo police car, stopped askew in the parking area with its rooftop red light still flashing, chattering away on two-way radios. They continued to harangue Lamar Argyle with inane questions and absurd commands. He not only refused to turn over Carlo Carlucci, he refused to move his police car, either to get it out of the way or to allow them to move Carlucci's car, which it blocked. Curious tourists congregated to rubberneck the ruction, and horseback cowboys from the arena rode over to watch.

Karen Harris looked on, an arm wrapped about Eric's shoulders. Rawhide Robinson returned to the disturbance and dispute, driving Eddie ahead like a plow mule (not that a cowboy would follow a plow, but the comparison is apt), his hands bound behind him with the borrowed lariat. He loosened the bonds and shoved the gangster into the back seat of Argyle's car and slammed the door. Coiling the rope, he spied its owner sitting aboard the once-borrowed horse among the inquisitive cowboys and returned it.

"What's goin' on?" the cowboy asked.

Rawhide Robinson said, "Them two scapegraces snatched the kid up in Alamo and brought him down here. Holed up and hid out in one of them hotel rooms. Don't know how Lamar—that's him, over there—he's the lawman in Alamo—flushed them out, on account of I was watchin' you-all headin' and heelin' those Mexican steers. Don't know what these other folks wants, but whatever it is Lamar ain't havin' any of it."

"You need any help, lemme know."

"Thanks, pard—and thanks again for the borrow of your horse and rope."

Rawhide Robinson walked back to Lamar's car and stood next to Karen and Eric. A golf cart threaded its way through the assembled onlookers, hauling a pair of men. One wore an expensive-looking business suit that gleamed in the sunlight. A big, fat pinky ring flashed on the hand grasping the post supporting the roof. The driver donned a top-stitched leisure suit with the collar of a loud shirt layered over the jacket's neckline. His neck also supported a heavy chain with a shiny medallion. Both wore dark glasses.

The leisure-suited driver beeped a horn and hollered "Make way" as he started and stopped and twisted and turned to guide the cart through the crowd. He braked to a stop next to the police car and his passenger stepped out.

"I can see why they wear them glasses," Rawhide Robinson said to Karen. "The shine on that feller's shoes could near blind you."

The man snapped the cuffs of his shirtsleeves then the lapels of his jacket and asked Lamar Argyle the same question the roper had asked Rawhide Robinson.

"I've arrested these two hoodlums for kidnapping," the police chief said.

"And just who the &$^@# are you?"

Lamar showed his badge and asked the same question, minus the profanity.

"Name's Clemenza. Head of Stardust security. That tin badge of yours says Alamo, Nevada."

"That's right."

"You're a little bit outside your jurisdiction, don't you think?"

Lamar's face fell as if he had not considered such a technicality. He soon recovered. "I reckon you're right. So let's just call this a citizen's arrest. I aim to hold them here until I can round up the local authorities."

"We'll see about that, flatfoot. You're on private property—as head of security here, it's my property. So you can just turn these men over to me and go on back to your hick town."

Clemenza's sunglasses did little to dim the intensity of the police chief's glare. He winced, although no one saw it.

"I don't think so," Lamar said.

The security man thumbed loose a button on his jacket and held it open, showing Argyle the black butt of a pistol in a shoulder holster. Lamar only smiled, but he moved his hand to rest upon the grip of the revolver hanging from his belt. Rawhide Robinson eased around the car to stand next to Argyle. When Carlo Carlucci started to rise from the back seat, Rawhide Robinson slowly pushed the car door closed, pinning the mobster's legs. Carlo sat back down.

The golf cart driver sidled up to Clemenza and whispered in his ear. His face reddened and his jaws clenched and unclenched. He stepped closer to the lawman. "Somebody called the cops. They're on their way," he said. "There's no need to involve them and this need not go any further. Why not let me take these men away and we'll call it even."

"Call it even?"

"Yeah. You won't be charged with trespassing, inciting a riot, assault, and anything else I can think of to hang on you."

Lamar laughed. "No thanks. I guess we'll let the police sort this out."

Clemenza smiled. "Fine. But let me warn you—you're making a big mistake."

Remembering his phone call to the Las Vegas Police about Karen's run-in with the mobsters, and how quickly the gangsters learned of it, Lamar realized it may well be a mistake. But he could not countenance letting Carlo and Eddie walk away from a kidnapping. The sound of approaching sirens told him the time for negotiation was past.

One after another, three Las Vegas Police Department prowl cars turned off the Strip and made their way to the parking area behind the Stardust. Six occupants climbed out of the cars and the onlookers parted to let them through.

"Clemenza," one of the policemen said.

"Sarge."

"What've we got here?" the LVPD sergeant said, eyes darting from the Stardust security guards to the woman and boy, the Alamo policeman, the cowboy, and Carlo and Eddie in the back of the out-of-town police car.

"Here's the thing, Sarge. This local yokel from Alamo came onto Stardust property uninvited and took two casino employees into custody, and caused no end of commotion in the process," Clemenza said. "As you see, he has caused a traffic hazard, he's preventing our guests from accessing their automobiles, and is behind this unlawful assembly!"

The LVPD sergeant rocked back and forth on his heels, hands clasped behind his back, as his eyes made another circuit. He stopped at Lamar Argyle. "You're a policeman?"

Argyle nodded.

"Is what he says true?"

"Some of it, I guess."

"Suppose you tell me what you think's going on here."

After a moment to collect his thoughts, Lamar said, "He's right that we came here uninvited." He pointed his chin at the gangster sitting on the back seat of his patrol car with his feet in the parking lot. "We followed this goon, Carlucci, here."

The dirty look the head of Stardust security sent Carlucci's way was almost visible through the dark lenses of his glasses. Carlo squirmed as if it struck him unfiltered.

"Why?"

"We thought he might lead us to Eric, there, and our hunch proved right. See, Carlucci and his pals Eddie and Spuds kidnapped the boy up in Alamo. And by the way—before I leave here I intend to arrest Spuds, as well."

The sergeant rocked on his heels some more. "We got no report of a kidnapping at LVPD. You report it?"

"Nope. Last time I talked to your department—in reference to the boy's mother, who these clowns also abducted, by the way—all it accomplished was to inform these bozos that the woman contacted me after they told her not to involve the police."

"You're saying someone in the department tipped them off?"

"Can't see it happening any other way."

"Best mind what you say. LVPD doesn't take too kindly to accusations of corruption."

Lamar shrugged.

"What happened when you got here?"

Lamar told how he watched Carlucci and Eddie enter one of the hotel rooms, then staked it out in hopes of spotting the boy. Spuds left the room and headed for the casino. One of the Stardust security guards laughed. "I bet you could find him in the buffet." The other guards joined in. Clemenza's wrathful, if shaded, eyes settled on the guards, cutting their laughter short.

Lamar said, "Karen—the boy's mother—went to use the facilities so I was on my own when Carlucci and Eddie shoved the boy out the door and followed him out. Looked like they meant to load him in the car and take him somewhere else. Eric, though, he ran off. Carlucci sent Eddie after him and followed in his car. I boxed him in right here where we sit.

"Eddie chased Eric out into that empty lot there. This cowboy here—he's with me, by the way—got himself a-horseback somehow and headed them off at the pass. Rescued the boy, then brought Eddie back trussed up like a calf at a branding."

That part of Lamar's story prompted a round of whistles and applause from the mounted cowboy onlookers.

The police sergeant kept rocking and looking around. After a time, "Clemenza, what about it? Looks to me like these boys of yours was up to something."

"Merely an attempt to collect a debt, Sarge. That's all. Carlo, he gets a little bit gung-ho sometimes. But kidnapping? No way! They got no proof. And like you said, it was never reported."

From out of the crowd stepped a man in a suit every bit as crisp and well-tailored as, but considerably less expensive than, that worn by Clemenza. His eyes, too, were concealed by sunglasses. "Yes, it was," the man said. "I took the report myself."

A tidal wave of shock and surprise passed through participants and onlookers alike. No one of them knew who this man was, where he came from, who sent him, or why he was here.

Chapter Thirty-Two

The man in the tailored suit pulled a wallet from his inside jacket pocket and flipped it open, displaying an identification card and gold badge. "Senior Special Agent Anderson," he announced, "Federal Bureau of Investigation." Behind Anderson, two other agents flashed their credentials.

"FBI?" the LVPD sergeant said. "Who called you?"

"It should come as no surprise to you, Sergeant, that the Bureau monitors police radio traffic."

"Fine. But why are you here?"

"Investigating a kidnapping. That, too, should not surprise you—pursuant to Title 18 of the United States Code, Subsection 120, kidnapping is a federal crime."

"Kidnapping? I've seen no report of any kidnapping."

"I have," the agent said. "As I said before, I took the report myself."

The police sergeant looked at Lamar Argyle. "You told me you didn't report a kidnapping."

The Alamo police officer nodded in agreement.

"You?" the sergeant said to Karen Harris.

She shook her head.

The LVPD sergeant turned back to the FBI agent. "It doesn't look like anybody here reported a kidnapping. So apparently you're not needed here, Senior Special Agent Anderson of the Federal Bureau of Investigation."

Anderson said to the boy, "Are you Eric Harris?"

"Ye—" the boy tried to say, losing the rest of the word in an involuntary swallow. "Y-yes," he said again, this time managing to iterate the entire syllable.

"That is the name of the kidnap victim as reported to me," the agent said to the sergeant.

"If you don't mind my asking, who, exactly, filed this report?"

"I am not at liberty to divulge the name, but I can tell you the report was filed by an employee of the federal government. An officer of the Central Intelligence Agency. He and two of his agents claim to have witnessed the abduction."

"Abduction!" Clemenza hollered. "There wasn't no abduction!"

"According to the CIA agents, an automobile that matches the description of the one parked right there, occupied by three men, snatched the Harris boy off an Alamo street and spirited him away in said automobile."

"Oh?" the sergeant said. "And just what were these government spies doing at the time they witnessed this so-called kidnapping?"

"Again, I am not at liberty to provide details. That information is a matter of national security. I can say, however, that they were on a stakeout with the intention of seizing a suspected trespasser."

Hearing those words, Rawhide Robinson eased away from the center of the action to stand among the cowboys gathered round to watch the spectacle.

"Agent Anderson, if I may," Lamar Argyle said. "Not only did these yahoos there in my car," he said, pointing out Carlo and Eddie, "abduct Eric, they kidnapped his mother, here, and held her hostage. And there's a third hoodlum involved—a big guy they call Spuds."

Carlo Carlucci pushed the car door aside and stood. "That ain't so!" he said, shaking his cuffed hands in the air. "I never kidnapped nobody!"

"Did so!" Eric yelled.

The FBI agent said, "Tell me what happened."

"Like you said—I was goin' to school. Walkin' along, y'know, minding my own business when this big, black car came rippin' past, flipped a u-ey, and Eddie, he got out and shoved me into the back of the car. Then they brought me here—stayed all night with Spuds in a room over there," he said, pointing at the hotel. "I got away twice—once in the casino, but they caught me, and I got away again, just now."

After Eric's story, the FBI agent questioned Karen about her experience with the three gangsters.

"Sounds like probable cause to me, Sergeant," Agent Anderson said. Then, to Lamar, "Mister Argyle, Chief Argyle, or whatever you prefer, I would appreciate your turning the two men in your custody over to the FBI. We'll take it from here."

The Alamo lawman complied, removed his handcuffs so one of the FBI agents could restrain Carlucci, and watched the ritual as the agents informed the hoodlums of their rights. Anderson instructed his agents to secure the captives in the agency vehicles then to track down and locate Spuds in the Stardust and arrest him.

"You're making a big mistake, Anderson," Clemenza said to the FBI agent. These men are in my employ and were only attempting to collect a debt, which is perfectly legal."

"I beg to differ, Mister Clemenza."

The Stardust security chief's eyes widened behind his dark glasses. "Who told you my name? I don't recall being introduced."

"Oh, the Bureau knows who you are, Mister Clemenza. Your picture—and those of several of your associates—is hanging on the wall over at our office. It is not on a 'wanted' poster yet—but I suspect it will be, soon enough."

"Sergeant!" Clemenza said to the police officer. "This man is threatening me! Do something—arrest him!"

The LVPD officer shook his head. "Sorry, Clemenza. He ain't said anything that would justify an arrest. Besides, no judge would hold him."

"Hmmph!" Clemenza said. "I know plenty of judges who'd lock him up on my say-so."

"Not this time," the sergeant said. He turned to the onlookers still hanging around. "Okay, folks, move along. Show's over. Nothing to see here." Then, "Argyle, move your car before I give you a ticket for illegal parking. Clemenza, have one of your men move this boat of Carlucci's out of here."

As the crowd dispersed, Lamar Argyle took Clemenza aside. "Look, mister," he said, "I know this ain't my jurisdiction. And, fact is, it ain't any of my business except that Miz Harris lives in my town. But I'm pokin' my nose in anyway."

"What is it you want, flatfoot?"

"Well, it's like this. Dwight Harris is dead. Died serving his country. Now, I know he died owing your place here money, but, like I said, he's dead and gone.

The money he lost in your casino ain't got nothing to do with his widow, nor the boy. They haven't got any money—only enough to barely get by up in Alamo. And, fact is, the Stardust probably makes a lot more money in ten minutes than what Dwight owed you. So why not let it go?"

Lamar couldn't discern Clemenza's reaction, his eyes hidden behind dark lenses. The security chief stood for a minute. He watched the FBI agents walking Spuds, in handcuffs, away from the casino and loading him into one of their cars. He watched the cowboys at Horseman's Park resume their roping contest. He watched the Las Vegas police officers shoo the remaining rubberneckers away. He watched Karen Harris wrap a protective arm around Eric's shoulder and guide him to the back seat of the Alamo police cruiser. He watched Rawhide Robinson walk up and stand to the side and a bit behind the Alamo police chief. Clemenza spoke. "You the cowboy that roped Eddie?"

"I am," Rawhide Robinson said.

"Pretty rough treatment, don't you think?"

The cowboy laughed. "No Sunday picnic, that's for sure. But I don't reckon his intentions toward the boy were any too honorable. Eric's a good boy. I didn't want to see him come to any harm. His ma, she's a good woman, too."

The gangster nodded. “My boys, they might have been overzealous.” He turned back to Lamar. “Okay, flatfoot. I’ll see what I can do to make Dwight Harris’s debt disappear. Now, the pair of you—get the @%#* off Stardust property. And don’t come back. Next time, I might not be in such a forgiving mood.”

The cowboy and the cop nodded, and climbed into the police car. As they drove out of the parking lot, the police sergeant waved him to a stop. As Lamar rolled down his window to see what he wanted, Senior Special Agent Anderson of the Federal Bureau of Investigation rolled his government sedan to a stop to the right of the car and signaled Rawhide Robinson to crank down his window.

The police sergeant said to Lamar, “You got lucky this time, town clown. You’d do well to keep in mind that it ain’t healthy to bet against the house in Las Vegas.”

The FBI agent said to Rawhide Robinson, “Tell me something, cowboy. By any chance do you ride a motorcycle?”

Chapter Thirty-Three

Rawhide Robinson watched another airliner sink for a landing as Lamar drove the Alamo patrol car out of Las Vegas. Farther on, he saw fighter jets darting around and diving into Nellis Air Force Base. He tipped back his thirteen-gallon hat and leaned down for a better look through the windows.

"Can't get over seein' them things fly around like that. It don't seem right, somehow."

Eric said from the back seat, "Those fighter jets, that's what my dad used to fly, y'know. I guess you haven't ever been in an airplane, have you, Rawhide."

The cowboy contemplated the rhetorical question. "No, son, I've never been in an airplane. But I did go flying one time."

Lamar's head snapped sideways to look at his passenger. Karen sat upright. Eric scooted forward and hooked his elbows over the back of the front seat. "Whaddya mean?"

Rawhide Robinson snapped the pull tab from a can of root beer and took a sip. He held up the can to admire the label. "I confess to having developed a taste for this here root beer. And these tin cans it comes in is right handy."

"C'mon, Rawhide! What about flying?"

"Take it easy, Eric. I'll give you the whole story from head to hock." Another sip. "Workin' a ranch job in Arizona, I was. Some cow work, but mostly they'd hired me on to snap out broncs for the cavvy. That outfit had more kinds of *caballos* than you can imagine—mustangs, Mexican horses, imported American horses from Back East, Indian ponies, Palouse horses, California *vaquero* horses, cayuses, Texas cow ponies—you name it. And, of course, crossbred equines of every kind.

"One fine summer day I was takin' the rough off some ponies. Beautiful afternoon, it was—light breeze takin' the edge off the heat. Sky as blue as Lord Byron's heaven, sprinkled with cotton-boll clouds."

Eric erupted. "Enough about the weather already!"

Rawhide Robinson smiled. "Well, I saddled up and rode six or seven steeds to a substantial sweat without incident. I was just gettin' good and warmed up when they run this one old pony into the breaker pen. And I do mean old. Must've been seven, maybe eight years old if he was a day. Now, I ain't got no notion how that horse came to be away down there near the border with Old Mexico, on account of he was a Percheron Puddin'

Foot from up Montana way if ever I saw one. But there he was. He stood in that pen eyein' me like I weren't nothin' more than a mouthful of sweet grass waiting to be et.

"Tall, he was—sixteen-and-a-half, seventeen hands maybe. Must have weighed in at 1500 pounds. Dapple gray. Deep chest like them Puddin' Foots show. Broad forehead, little pin ears, big eyes. Heavy hooves—I remember imaginin' how it would feel to have one of them feet planted in the middle of my breadbasket."

"Rawhide!" Eric said. "You're s'posed to be telling about flying, y'know. You've been yakking about the weather and this horse—what's that got to do with anything?"

"I'm comin' to it."

Lamar piped up, "Well, get to it. The boy makes a good point."

"Have you-all ever heard of that French play writer called Molière?"

A trio of "no" came in response.

"Well, he once said, 'Trees that are slow to grow bear the best fruit.' You-all might take that sagacity to heart and allow me to tell my own story."

Waiting a moment, then two, then three for the wisdom to take root, Rawhide Robinson continued. "That horse stood like a statue while I cinched down the saddle. I took ahold of the cheek piece and cranked his head around, found the stirrup—which was a stretch, given the height of that horse—and stepped onto the hurricane deck.

"He stood there all aquiver till I tickled his gizzard with my gut hooks. Then he stuck his bill in the ground and boiled over. Talk about buck—that horse was a high roller, a sunfisher, a pile-driver, and he did the double shuffle. When he slatted his sails he could buck on a dime, swap ends, suck back, and windmill. He pump-handled, crow-hopped, cow-kicked, jackknifed, and pawed at the clouds.

"I'll tell you, boys—you too, Miz Karen—I weathered that storm for a time, but it was all I could do to keep from grabbin' the apple and pulling leather. After a while I took to rattling loose and showing daylight. Then that horse hid his head and broke his back and the soles of my boots saw sunlight. 'Fore you know it, I was coming down and he was goin' up and we met in the middle—and that launched me like one of them there aeroplanes we seen. Sent me flying, he did," Rawhide Robinson said, and sipped his root beer.

"That's it?!" Eric said.

Lamar said, "You got thrown by a horse!?"

"That's what you call flying?" Karen said.

Rawhide Robinson smiled, then again tipped and lipped his root beer can.

The diatribe of disappointment, chorus of frustration, denunciation of disgruntlement continued for a time until the cowboy hefted a hand, signaling for silence. With his audience once again in hand, he said, "Like it or not, believe it or no, I tell you I was flying that day. But that ain't the half of it. As any bronc stomper will tell you, getting bucked off ain't no big thing. Don't hurt a bit.

"Landing, now, that's where the trouble comes. Eating dirt, chewing gravel, biting the dust, kissing the ground, landing on your hat—ain't none of 'em enjoyable. As I kept flying up and up, I took to contemplatin' how bad coming down was going to be. I was a-flying higher and higher and got to where I found myself amongst them cotton-boll clouds I told you about. And, lo and behold, just as I reached the apex of my arc and reversed course, I lit right atop one of them clouds. I'm here to tell you, as much as a cloud might look like cotton, when you land on one it's even softer—more like a plump eider-down pillow."

The revelation spurred vocalizations of incredulity.

"I tell you it's true. Still, as soft as that cloud was, it was as bouncy as a bedspring. So before I knowed what was happening, I was expelled from that cloud and on the fly again. And it kept on happening—I was bounced from one cloud to another, clean across the sky. I swear I'd be up there still, had I not flown and floated from one puffy pillow to the next until I got to a place where them clouds kissed the peaks of the Huachuca Mountains. So, I just stepped off onto a mountaintop and headed on back to the ranch on the hoof."

Groans and grumbling, gripes and grousing, guff and grievances greeted the cowboy raconteur at the conclusion of his chronicle. Undaunted and unruffled, Rawhide Robinson emptied his root beer can into his oral cavity. Once calm returned to the car, the cowboy asked a question: "What about Eric's machine?"

Chapter Thirty-Four

The tall sign at Betty's Coyote Springs Ranch first appeared as a dim blur on the horizon, then a landmark in the anonymous emptiness, and, finally, as a beckoning finger touting tantalizing, titillating, taboo thrills. As Lamar Argyle turned the Alamo police car into the parking lot, Karen Harris clapped a hand over Eric's eyes in a vain attempt to protect him from the realities of rural Nevada's uncommon attractions.

"Mom!" he said, swiping the hand away. "We're just getting my motorcycle, y'know! It ain't like we're customers."

"Eric!"

The decision to rescue the motorbike was a considered one. There were only two drivers' licenses in the patrol car. Neither Lamar nor Karen knew how to operate the motorbike, and Rawhide Robinson did not advise learning on the fly, as he had been forced to do. The cowboy volunteered to pilot the machine, but his lack of credentials offered no advantage vis-à-vis Eric, nor was he as experienced or proficient a driver as the boy.

Lamar's means of getting the motorcycle back to Alamo was simple: Eric would ride the bike, the police would follow with red light flashing. Then, in the unlikely event they might encounter the state police or county sheriff on patrol, Eric would pull over and the Alamo police chief would claim he had the infraction and the malefactor under control.

Seeing the patrol car in the parking lot, Betty came out to say hello. Intent on Eric's motorcycle machinations, neither Lamar nor Rawhide Robinson nor Karen was aware of her presence until she knocked on the glass of the passenger-side window.

"I do declare—it's Mister Rawhide Robinson," she said as he rolled down the window.

"Howdy, Miz Betty."

"Lamar."

"Betty."

The madam glanced into the back seat, but Karen's bowed-down red face offered no acknowledgement.

"You boys comin' in for a drink? Cup of coffee?"

"No thanks, Betty," Lamar said. "We've got to get back to Alamo." He looked over to where Eric readied the motorcycle. Instead, the boy stood slack-jawed, eyes on the madam. "Eric! You ready to go?"

The boy's face turned florid, a shade matching that of his mother's. "Yes, sir, Mister Argyle." He swung a leg over the motorbike, pushed it off the kickstand, turned the key, twisted the throttle grip, and stood on the kick starter. It took three tries before the engine growled to life. Eric set off for the highway, looking back over his shoulder for a final glimpse of Betty.

Betty waved at the boy, then said, "Well, Rawhide, the girls will be sorry they missed you. I swear, they haven't shut up about your stories. You're welcome here anytime."

"Thank you, ma'am. Give my regards to the ladies."

"Lamar."

"Betty," the lawman said as he slipped the car into gear and swung it around in the gravel parking lot and followed Eric onto the highway.

Traffic, as usual, was light on Highway 93. Karen shivered each time Eric and the motorbike shuddered when a tractor-trailer passed, but the trip went off without a hitch. As they passed the Pahranaghet lakes and Alamo appeared, Rawhide Robinson said, "You know, I got me a hankering for one of them cheeseburger sandwiches." He thumbed one of the redeemable souvenir chips from Betty's Coyote Springs Ranch. "I don't suppose these things are legal tender."

"Likely not," Lamar said with a laugh. "You might luck out and sell one to a truck driver. But I don't think the Wagon Wheel café would give you a burger for it."

"I'll buy," Karen said. "If you'll put that thing away."

Lamar laughed again. “I’ll buy—leastways, the police department budget will. We been on police business, so I believe the town board will find it a legitimate expenditure of taxpayer dollars.”

They turned off the highway onto Weeping Willow Street and followed Eric as he doubled back onto Fehringer Road for home. Soon, Eric was in the back seat with his mother and they were on their way to the local bean parlor. The hang-abouts and regulars at the restaurant greeted Rawhide Robinson by name, and recognized the police chief. The proprietor came around with menus.

Rawhide Robinson pushed the bill of fare aside and said, “I believe I’m hungry enough to eat a saddle blanket. That not being on the board, how’s about you bring me one of them cheeseburgers. And I’ll wash it down with a cup of hot java and a cool root beer, if you please.”

As his tablemates looked on with amusement, the cowboy took pleasure in the novelty—for him, at least—of ketchup and mustard in squeeze bottles and the jukebox with its tabletop selectors pouring out music in exchange for a coin in the slot while they ate. He did not know what to think of the songs Eric selected—he called the music rock and roll—but since Lamar and

Karen seemed equally flummoxed, he determined his quandary had more to do with age than the age.

Sitting back with a satisfied smile at the conclusion of the meal, Rawhide Robinson yawned and rubbed his eyes. "If I had my bedroll, I believe I'd unspool it right here and check my eyelids for leaks. I did not sleep long nor well in that motor buggy of yours, Marshal."

"It has been a long day. I'll take you folks back home, then I intend to put my feet up and relax. If I make it to bedtime with my eyes open, I'll be surprised."

At home, Karen questioned Eric about his captivity. The boy seemed none the worse for wear from the adventure. He was more interested in how his motorcycle came to be parked at Betty's Coyote Springs Ranch. "Y'know, I guess you didn't realize what it would do to my reputation if anyone recognized it parked there."

"I'm awful sorry, son," Rawhide Robinson said. "You afraid folks might think poorly of you for consorting with soiled doves?"

Eric laughed. "Heck no! I'd be a hero at school! The guys in my class would worship me."

"Eric!" his mother said.

"Oh, Mom!"

"You have no business talking about such things. Not at your age."

"Yeah, right. I'm not a kid anymore, Mom."

"No. you're not. You've reached the ripe old age of fourteen. Practically a senior citizen. Keep it up, and you won't make fifteen. Go to bed. You've got school tomorrow."

"School? Mom, I'm recovering from being kid-napped. I'm traumatized. I could go over the edge at any time, y'know."

"What are you saying?"

"I can't possibly go to school tomorrow. The kids would kill me with questions."

"Oh, Eric! They can't possibly know what hap-pened."

"Are you kidding, Mom? This is Alamo. You can't go to the bathroom in this town without everybody knowing about it!"

Karen employed all forty-three of her facial muscles in an unsuccessful attempt to keep from smiling. "All right. One day. But that's it—one day. Then it's back to school."

"Okay, Mom. I'll try to hold it together. But I'm on the thin edge here, y'know."

"Goodnight, Eric. I don't have the luxury of a day off to recover. I've got to go to work in the morning."

Eric and Rawhide Robinson spent the rest of the evening staring at the television set. Despite the fact that the programs featured so-called cowboys who seldom—

if ever—crossed paths with a cow, the artificial Old West settings evoked in the ordinary—but real—cowboy a wistfulness, a loneliness, and a longing for home—if not a place, at least a time.

The boy drifted off to bed and Rawhide Robinson tugged off his boots and stretched out on the sofa.

Across the street and down the road, a dark sedan pulled out of the space between parked farm implements and rolled slowly down the street toward town. A CIA agent stepped out at the phone booth in front of the Wagon Wheel café and dialed the operator, a handful of coins at the ready.

Miles away, the phone rang in the quarters of the man in the rumpled suit, now dressed in pajamas and watching a Western on TV while he smoked the last cigarette of the evening. He picked up the phone and the voice on the other end of the line said, “He’s here.”

Chapter Thirty-Five

P-B-and-J sandwiches were on the breakfast menu at the Harris household. Eric and Rawhide Robinson sat at the kitchen table, the boy lubricating his mouth with milk and the cowboy with coffee. Already at work at the bank, Karen had left early to catch up on the work that piled up in her absence. The cowboy was quiet, staring at something through the window glass that held his interest.

"What's the matter, Rawhide?"

"Oh! Nary a thing, son," he said with a start.

"Whatcha thinking about?"

The cowboy's interest in the window shifted to his coffee mug. "I don't know. Nothing—everything. Whole world's gone plumb loco. I've seen things of late that make me think I've gone loco. Ain't been off a horse for this long since I can't even remember when. Don't know if I'd recognize a cow if it swatted me with its switch."

"But you were on that horse when you roped Eddie."

"I reckon you're right. But that weren't for but a minute. It don't hardly count."

Eric laughed. "It counted if you ask me. That goon mighta killed me, y'know."

"Oh, I don't know. I think that boy was as thick in the head as feathers in a pillow. He only did what Carlo told him. Carlo, he knowed your daddy—God rest his soul—owed their outfit money but he didn't have no clue what to do about it. Didn't think no more about grabbing you nor your ma than a frog thinks about fandangos."

"I guess so. But I was scared all the same."

"Don't blame you. But you was right smart tryin' to get away. Brave, too. Showed you got gravel in your gizzard."

Eric reddened and said nothing for half a sandwich. "So what are you going to do now, Rawhide?"

Rawhide Robinson stretched and yawned, extended his legs under the table, leaned back in his chair, and laced his fingers behind his head. "Wish I knew, Eric. Wish I knew."

"Go home, maybe?"

A laugh. "When you're a cowboy, home is wherever you spread your blanket." He sat up and propped his elbows on the table. "Last place I called home was the 51 Ranch."

Eric squirmed. "I don't see how that can be."

"Me neither. I confess to being as confused as a snake in a shoe store." He finished his coffee and gathered his mug and Eric's glass and carried them to the sink. "I'm thinkin' of maybe going back out there."

"But you know there's nothing to see—just a bunch of old boards and some beer cans."

"I know it. Seeing it in the daylight might make a difference, somehow. Maybe not. But I ain't got nothin' else to hold onto."

Eric, ever up for adventure, offered to drive the quixotic cowboy on his motorcycle. He left a note for his mother in case they were late getting back, filled a canteen, poured gas from a five-gallon can into the motorbike's tank, and set out on desert backroads for the former location of the 51 Ranch.

And the suburbs of Area 51.

Stubbing out yet another cigarette, the CIA man brushed ashes from the lapels of his disheveled suit coat. The military man, as starched as the CIA man was wrinkled, sat across the expanse of his immaculate desk, eyeing with disdain the scattering of ashes radiating from ground zero of the ash tray. He steepled his fingers and leaned back in his swivel chair, eying the operative over the top of his eyeglasses.

"You remain convinced the man must be caught."

The CIA man clicked and clicked the button on his ballpoint pen. “Yes. I’ve always said so. The longer he remains out there, the more risk he represents.”

“But you have nothing to back up your contention. All reports say he has disclosed nothing about our work here.”

“Not quite. Area 51 did come up in his discussions at the Boot Hill Bar in Alamo.”

The military man smiled, even chuckled a bit. “Yes. And from what I am told, it was the patrons of the bar spouting the usual stories about space aliens and flying saucers and the like.”

“True enough. But he did go to Las Vegas—or so we believe.” The CIA man lit another cigarette. “Who knows what he might have got up to there? Newspapers, investigators, foreign agents, for all we know.”

Again, the military man smiled. “For all we know, he doesn’t know anything.”

Ejecting a stream of smoke that drifted halfway across the desk before dissipating, the CIA man said, “We know he saw the A-12. He’d have to be blind not to—it practically ran over him!”

“True. But all indications are that he didn’t—doesn’t—know what he was looking at.”

“Indications? What indications?”

"You know full well—you saw the psychiatrist's report. He says the man is seriously delusional."

"Of course he does—what do you expect a shrink to say? His job is to tag everybody with one form of 'osis' or another."

"Still, it's the best we've got so far."

"Which is exactly why we need to apprehend the cowboy. That doctor turned him loose before he was properly debriefed. We won't know what he knows—or what he may have disclosed, even inadvertently—until he's properly interrogated. Think about it—we don't even know how he ended up at Groom Lake in the first place!"

"The physicists—"

"Physicists! Wormholes! Are you kidding? You can't possibly believe what those eggheads are saying! If you do, you're—"

"—I will remind you who you are talking to. Mind what you say."

"I'm sorry, Sir. But I attach the utmost urgency to this matter." He smashed the remnants of the latest cigarette into the ashtray. "Now, we know he was back in Alamo last night. All I'm saying is that we bring him in and get him properly vetted. If we determine there's no risk, we'll turn him loose."

"Or, turn him over to the physicists."

"Even I wouldn't countenance that. Who knows what kind of lame-brained experiment they've got cooked up."

The military man removed his glasses and massaged the bridge of his nose. "We'll cross that bridge when we come to it. Go ahead and apprehend him—if you can do it quietly. I do not want any public outcry over the seizure of this cowboy."

The CIA man clicked the ballpoint pen and slid it into his shirt pocket. Within minutes, he and two of his operatives were in a nondescript sedan, heading for the Groom Lake Road and the town of Alamo.

Chapter Thirty-Six

Dust and tumbleweeds, trash and cheat grass littered the site. The unforgiving glare of the desert sun flared on discarded beer cans and shattered bottles. Sagging posts and collapsed rails and broken boards defined the outlines of long-gone pens and corrals.

"Ain't no doubt this is 51 headquarters," Rawhide Robinson said. "Or was."

Eric watched as Rawhide Robinson paced and paused, wandered and stopped, shaking his head in disbelief at what, only days before, had been a hardscrabble but working cattle ranch.

"Yonder there, that's where the bunkhouse sat. Barn ain't but a few scraps of old lumber now. You can see where the main house was; them jumbled stones is what's left of the foundation." The cowboy shuffled his way around and around the area again and again, pointing out this and that, searching for something sensible but finding only shadows.

And confusion.

He could not even find a cow track or print from a horseshoe—nothing but tread marks from motorcycle, automobile, and truck tires marred the ranch yard. And instead of road apples and pasture flapjacks littering the ground, he found only refuse from beer busts and booze bashes.

One thing was certain. The 51 Ranch was long gone. And, it seemed to the perplexed, perturbed, puzzled, nonplussed, stumped, befuddled, and bewildered buckaroo, so was the whole world as he knew it.

Eric scuffed at the ground with his toe. "I don't know what to tell you, Rawhide. It's always been this way as far as I know. There's other ranches around where some of my friends live, but this is…well, y'know, it's just this."

"I can see that—and that's what makes it so all-fired baffling. But it ain't just this—it's everything. Whole world's gone loco, and even if I could throw a loop around it I wouldn't know whether to dally up or tie off."

"I feel real bad…."

"Oh, it ain't your fault, Eric. Fact is, if you hadn't come along I don't know what would've become of me. You've stuck with me like spots on a pinto horse and I'm obliged to you for that. 'Course I didn't think so, that first night you talked me into straddling that contraption of yours. I thought you was tryin' to kill me."

Eric laughed. "Look at you now—you even learned to drive it."

"Oh, no—I managed to herd that thing down the road, but I can't say I got it broke to ride. And if it's all the same to you, I won't be takin' up the reins again."

The sound of a car on the gravel road interrupted the conversation and they watched a dark sedan pass on the way to Alamo, kicking up pebbles and a wispy trail of dust. The dust billowed into a cloud when brakes locked the wheels and the car skidded to a stop. The car reversed, stopped again, then wheeled off the road into the former ranch yard to stop near Eric's parked motorbike. Both front doors and the left rear door on the sedan swung open and three men in suits stepped out.

The driver, whose suit looked like he had slept in it, pinched a cigarette from his mouth and flicked the ash off the end. "Rawhide Robinson, unless I'm mistaken."

The cowboy nodded. Eric took a step backward and eased behind Rawhide Robinson as the other two men from the car fanned out to the sides.

"Say," the cowboy said. "I know you—you're one of them Area 51 folks."

"That's right. I questioned you after you were found wandering around on Groom Lake," the CIA man said. He dropped his cigarette butt and ground it out in the dirt with the toe of his dusty shoe.

"You tried to shoot me, too. Right after them gangsters grabbed ol' Eric here."

"Well, I'm awful sorry about that. The thing is, I've got more questions."

Rawhide Robinson laughed. "Between you and that other man I pow-wowed with out there, I flapped my jaw enough to stir up a dust devil. I told him everything I know and then some."

"Be that as it may, Mister Robinson, we'd appreciate your coming with us."

Eric stepped forward. "Why? What're you gonna do, do some of your wacky experiments on him?"

The CIA man laughed.

"I've heard what you guys do out there!"

"Don't believe everything you hear, kid."

"Yeah, right. If you guys ain't up to something, why's it all so secret? What are you trying to hide?"

Fishing a pack of cigarettes out of his shirt pocket, the CIA man shook one out, touched the flame of his Zippo lighter to it, and inhaled a long, deep draft of smoke. He looked at the boy, then at the cowboy, then back at the boy.

"Suffice it to say we are engaged in research and testing vital to our national defense." The CIA man looked back at the cowboy. "Now, Mister Robinson—shall we go?"

Tipping his thirteen-gallon hat back and hitching his thumbs in his vest, the cowboy said, “And just supposin’ I don’t want to go?”

“Why wouldn’t you?”

“I said ‘suppose.’ Don’t mean I won’t. But you folks ain’t exactly been hospitable. Pointing guns at me. Locking me in little rooms. Chasing after me. Threatening me. You must have nothing under your hat but hair if you believe I’ll tie my horse to the back of your wagon and ride along just for the fun of it.”

“I understand your reluctance—”

“—Well, it ought not be too difficult. The reasons why are as plain as the hump on a camel.”

The CIA man raised a hand to restrain the cowboy’s objection. “I understand your reluctance, but I’m afraid I have to insist. Besides, I believe it could be to your benefit.”

“Oh? How’s that?”

“According to our researchers—well, two of them, a couple of physicists—there’s a chance, just a chance mind you, but a chance—we may be able to get you back to where you belong.”

Rawhide Robinson lit up like a coal-oil lantern. “That right?”

“Like I said, they say there’s a chance.”

The cowboy pursed his lips, wrinkled his forehead, squinted his eyes, and tried to restrain the stampede inside his skull.

"But," the CIA man said.

"But?"

"It—whatever it is the eggheads have in mind—won't happen if you don't come with us back to the base."

Eric leaned toward Rawhide Robinson and whispered, "Don't do it. Don't go."

The cowboy's eyes widened and he said, "Why not?"

"Who knows what they'll do to you? Y'know, I've heard people don't come back from out there."

"Aah, Eric. There ain't no need to worry none. As interesting as it's been these past few days with you-all, I don't belong here. The way I see it, no matter what happens out there it can't be no worse. The world is already as crazy as a mama cow lookin' for a lost calf.

"Now, you fork that machine of yours and go on back to town. Tell your ma I thank her kindly for the hospitality, and let that lawman Lamar know I'm obliged for all he done for me." Rawhide Robinson wrapped an arm around Eric's shoulders and gave him a squeeze. "And should you happen to run across Carlo or any of his goons, you tell him if he gives you or your mother any trouble, I'll kick him in the backside so hard he'll be wearin' his pants for a hat."

With another squeeze of the boy's shoulders, Rawhide Robinson turned Eric loose and walked to the car. "Well, boys," he said as he lifted and reset his thirteen-gallon hat then tugged it down tight. "Let's go."

Chapter Thirty-Seven

Dusty wingtip shoes and scuffed high-heeled boots echoed down the long, narrow hallway. The cowboy and a cloud of cigarette smoke followed the CIA man down the passage. Whether they were on the same subterranean level below the tin buildings at Groom Lake as before or on another, Rawhide Robinson did not know. As before, they turned into one of a number of identical doorways lining the hall. But rather than a cramped interrogation room like the cowboy had seen before, this time they passed through an anteroom and into a conference room. The psychiatrist sat at one end of the table, the military officer at the center of the table's long side. Rawhide Robinson and the CIA man took seats opposite.

The military man tapped at the edges of a stack of already perfectly aligned pages sitting next to a file folder on the table before him. "Rawhide Robinson, as I recall," he said. The cowboy nodded in reply. "I understand you have had quite an adventure since leaving us." Again, the cowboy nodded. "Do you know why you are here, Mister Robinson?"

"No, Sir. And call me Rawhide."

"Rawhide, then. Area 51—the United States Air Force facility you somehow stumbled into—is a classified military operation. Which means mere presence here requires high-level security clearance from the government."

"What you're saying is, it's a big secret."

"I suppose that is an accurate observation. But it is much more complicated than that. Tell me, Mister Ro—Rawhide, what do you know about our work here?"

The cowboy laughed and tipped back his thirteen-gallon hat with the touch of a finger. "Can't say as I know anything. I've heard a passel of things, most of which don't mean hide nor hair to me."

"Such as?"

"Oh, folks talk about you-all hiding out little men from outer space and flying saucers and such. Fiddlin' with the weather. Making stuff disappear. Stuff like that."

"Do you believe these things?"

Rawhide Robinson laughed. "Truth is, the things I've seen these past few days make me wonder if my thinker has pulled its picket pin and gone astray. I don't believe half of what I've seen with my own eyes."

The military man again straightened the already-straight pile of papers on the table. He looked at the CIA man who sat next to Rawhide Robinson, clicking a ballpoint pen and smoking a cigarette. The agent brushed ash from his lapels and said, "What about here at the base? What, exactly, have you seen here?"

"You mean besides these little rooms and soldiers pointing guns at me?"

The CIA man nodded.

"Well, not long after I woke up and found my horse missing, I started off across that playa out there to get back to the ranch. Somethin' the size of a freight train and making even more noise came a-flying over my head. Scared the holes right off my socks. It landed out there and turned around like it was comin' after me, but turned into one of them big buildings out there instead. That's about it."

"Do you remember what this thing looked like?"

"Not much. It was long and skinny and had pointy things in front. Never seen anything like it before."

"What did you think it was?"

"Hadn't no idea whatsoever," Rawhide Robinson said, removing his hat and raking his fingers through his hair. He reset the hat, then said, "'Course now I know it was some kind of airplane."

The CIA man sat up straight and stared at the cowboy. The clicking of the pen increased until he set it aside to light a fresh cigarette. "How do you know that?"

"Saw some when we went down there to Las Vegas. Lamar Argyle—the lawman there in Alamo—and Eric's mother Karen told me all about them. But the one I saw out here didn't look anything like them. Whole different deal, I'd have to say."

The military man cleared his throat. "Did you mention the airplane you saw here to anyone?"

Thinking and remembering furrowed Rawhide Robinson's forehead and pursed his lips. "Don't believe so."

Sliding the stack of pages into the folder, the uniformed man said, "I believe we're finished here, gentlemen. I do not believe Mister Rob—Rawhide represents any threat to our security."

"Are you sure, Sir?" the CIA man said.

"I am. It seems clear he has no information that could compromise any of our missions here." He turned his attention to the cowboy. "Now, Rawhide, the question is, what do we do with you?"

Rawhide Robinson pointed his chin at the CIA man and said to the military man, "This feller here, he says you-all might have a way to get me back where I belong."

The military man stood and tucked the folder under his arm. " 'Might' most likely overstates the case, I am afraid. I will summon the physicists. Gentlemen," he said and left the room.

The psychiatrist, silent until now, said, "Rawhide? I have a few questions I'd like to ask while we wait."

"Shoot."

To the CIA man, "Do you mind leaving us? Patient confidentiality, you know."

"Not on your life, doctor. Last time you were left alone with this man you released him. That won't happen again."

"You're perfectly welcome to wait in the other room. If we attempt to sneak past you, you are perfectly welcome to apprehend us on the spot."

"Hmmph," the intelligence operative said. He stubbed out his cigarette and left the room, closing the door with more force than necessary.

Once alone, the psychiatrist scribbled notes as he asked the cowboy to recount his adventures of the past days, interrupting with questions about his fascination with motor vehicles and bright lights and condiments in squeeze bottles; his impressions of refrigerators and television sets and showgirls; his enjoyment of cheeseburgers and peanut butter and jelly sandwiches and root beer; his astonishment at casinos and resort hotels and a big city with no particular reason for its existence.

"And then there are all them airplanes," Rawhide Robinson said.

"What about them?"

"Well, them flying at all is a wonder."

The psychiatrist nodded. "In your experience, then, no one ever even imagined such a thing?"

"No, I reckon not. Oh, a few years ago down in Texas there was this Dutchman name of Brodbeck who built what he called a flying machine. All he managed to do was get the thing off the ground long enough to crash it into a chicken coop. But them airplanes gettin' up and down with more'n a hundred folks in them—I don't see how anyone could think of doing that, let alone make it work. I'll tell you one thing, though—you won't catch this cowboy in one of them things. Broncs have tossed me as high in the sky as I care to be."

"So what do you think of this world you've found yourself in?"

Again, thought and consideration and reflection altered the cowboy's physiognomy. After a few moments, he said, "It's a heck of a thing, Doc. It's kind of like a dream, I suppose. Nothing's quite right, if you know what I mean. Oh, folks ain't much different—there's good and bad, like you'd expect. But everything else is a mite off kilter. Even the stuff I recognize ain't quite right. Somehow, I don't belong here no more than sheep on a cattle ranch."

"One other thing, Rawhide—these stories you tell."

The cowboy grinned. "What about 'em?"

Hemming and hawing and hesitating, the doctor finally managed to ask whether Rawhide Robinson believed they were true.

"True? Of course they're true." The cowboy let that sink in, then said, "'But that don't mean they happened just exactly like I say. See, it ain't no different than them stories on the television. That nonsense on there ain't got no more to do with what cowboyin' is like than a bronc peeler bouncin' on a cloud—if you know what I mean," he said with a sly smile.

The psychiatrist scribbled more notes on his pad and grinned back at the cowboy.

A tap on the door announced its opening, and it swung wide as the CIA man entered. The scientists breezed through behind him, white lab coats flowing like wizards' capes. The younger of the two was all smiles as he used his index finger to slide his spectacles up the bridge of his nose.

The older one, all business, glanced at the clipboard in his hand and said, "Well, Mister Robinson, are you ready to go home?"

Chapter Thirty-Eight

Mimicking the physical properties of a gas, the enthusiasm of the physicists expanded until it filled the conference room. The men in their white lab coats unfolded an easel to prop up a portable chalkboard. Accompanied by a deluge of meaningless words, the younger of the two rat-tat-tatted indecipherable rows of symbols and figures and numerals and letters on the board, periodically wiping out some or all with an eraser and launching another barrage. So exuberant was his notation that chalk dust drifted in Brownian motion through the room's energized air.

The onslaught continued for several minutes until Rawhide Robinson, wide-eyed and pale-faced, raised a hand. "Uh, gentlemen," he said.

Stopping the chalk mid-stroke, the younger of the scientists turned and said, "Yes?"

"That stuff you're writing there. It don't make a lick of sense to me. I can read just fine, but that looks like something a flock of chickens scratched out in a barnyard."

The physicists stared at each other, as baffled as the cowboy.

The psychiatrist mentioned the cryptic nature of the equations to an audience untrained in the finer points of physics.

The CIA man shared a similar opinion, albeit with less decorum. “Why don’t you two eggheads cut the crap and tell us what you want to do. In plain English,” he said.

Sliding his spectacles up the bridge of his nose with an index finger, the younger scientist sat in a convenient chair, perplexed and puzzled. The older man removed his eyeglasses and scrubbed the lenses with the tail of his lab coat, paying no attention to the process, his mind occupied elsewhere and his eyes seeing nothing. After a minute or two, during which he must have abraded countless silica molecules from the lenses with his absent-minded wiping, he replaced the spectacles on his face and likewise took a seat.

The senior scientist swallowed hard and said, “I will do my best. But be forewarned that the nature of our experiment involves hypotheses and concepts so enmeshed in the field of theoretical physics that they cannot be easily explained in common parlance—descriptive language, in many cases, simply does not exist, even metaphorically.”

"Well, do what you can," the intelligence officer in the rumpled suit said, lighting a fresh cigarette. "We'll try to keep up."

"As you may recall, we are of the opinion that we find Mister Robinson among us owing to his being thrust through an Einstein-Rosen Bridge, or so-called wormhole, as a result of a lightning strike. We believe we can reverse the process."

"You mean send me back?" Rawhide Robinson said.

"Precisely."

"Hold on a minute," the CIA man said. "You mean to tell me you really believe this cowboy is a time traveler?"

The elder physicist hemmed and hawed and shuffled his feet. "That cannot be determined for certain by science. At least not by physics. We can only interpret and analyze his reports of events and use that as a basis for our conclusions and as a framework for proposing corrective action."

"Hmmph," was the reply, accompanied by a few decisive clicks of a ballpoint pen.

"Psychiatry is a science—of a different kind, for sure—but science nonetheless," the psychiatrist said, sucking the stem of his pipe as he lit it. "And it is my scientific opinion that Rawhide Robinson is, indeed, a man out of his time."

The CIA man pointed out the doctor's earlier contention that the cowboy was simply insane.

"You're right. I did say that. I thought so at the time. But based on further discussions with the subject, I am convinced he does not belong in our day and age. His intelligence is beyond question, but his awareness of the modern world is nonexistent. I would describe this lack of knowledge as innocence, rather than ignorance, as he has shown a remarkable ability to adapt to unfamiliar circumstances. And need I remind you that you, yourself, used the potential of a return home to persuade Robinson to come in with you."

The CIA man clicked his pen. "I did. But it was only a ploy to convince him to come along. I didn't believe it then, and I don't believe it now. Do you?"

Squirming in his seat, the psychiatrist mulled over his answer. "We're walking on unfamiliar ground here in terms of psychiatry, physics, or, for that matter, our basic understanding of what reality is. But, as I said, I see no other explanation."

Rawhide Robinson followed the discussion with a bemused look, as the conversation concerning him continued as if he were not present.

"So, your recommendation is to turn him over to these lab rats?" the CIA man said.

"Can you recommend an alternative?"

The CIA man did not even have to think about it. "Lock him up."

"For what?"

"Trespassing. Divulging government secrets. Evading arrest. I could go on."

The doctor laughed. "But you have no evidence he committed those crimes—or any others, as far as that goes."

"But we found him wandering around on Groom Lake. If that's not trespassing, I don't know what is!"

"For trespassing to be unlawful, it requires a person to knowingly enter or encroach upon another person's property without permission."

"So?"

"So, Rawhide did no such thing. In the first place, he did not come to be here 'knowingly.' And, second, you cannot identify how, when, or even where he entered Area 51."

"Hmmmph."

"Furthermore, you have no evidence that he disclosed any secret or classified information to anyone. And without evidence of a crime, your accusations of evading arrest are ludicrous."

Click, click, click went the ballpoint pen in the CIA man's hand. He dropped it on the table, stubbed out his cigarette, and reached for a fresh one—pausing momentarily to brush the ashes from his lapels. "What does the United States Air Force have to say about all this?"

The younger physicist shoved his glasses higher on his nose. "We've been given a tentative go-ahead. Most of the preparations have been made. All that remains is to schedule time with the boys at the particle accelerator." Even as he spoke those two final words, the young scientist realized his mistake. His jaw fell open, His eyes widened. A hand covered his mouth. His eyes darted to his superior, who returned a heated, if helpless, glare.

"Accelerator? What accelerator?" the CIA man said, exhaling a cloud of smoke and retrieving his pen.

"I'm sorry, Sir. I've said too much."

The CIA man looked from one physicist to the other. "We have a particle accelerator here? Where?"

Clearing his throat, the senior scientist said, "We are not at liberty to divulge that information. Classified."

"What!? I am the Central Intelligence Agency Station Chief. I have the highest security clearance there is! I know things about you two that you don't even know about yourselves. So don't tell me it's classified!"

"In this case, I'm afraid, your security clearance is insufficient. But since the cat is out of the bag, so to speak; since my colleague has spilled the beans, run off at the mouth, gone off half-cocked, let it slip, or however you care to phrase it, I will elaborate—to a point. What I say cannot leave this room. Am I clear?"

In turn, the CIA man, psychiatrist, and cowboy agreed to hold secret the forthcoming information.

Chapter Thirty-Nine

First checking the anteroom to assure their privacy, the senior physicist turned the lock on the doorknob and launched a basic—from his standpoint—explanation of accelerators and colliders and quantum mechanics and particle physics. The CIA man objected, claiming such information superfluous, but the scientist carried on. The three members of the audience endured the lecture, eyes glassed over and understanding overwhelmed.

An occasional comment interrupted the stream. Rawhide Robinson, for example, expressed surprise at the very existence of anything smaller than an atom. He seemed to recall reading somewhere, sometime, about atoms, the basic building blocks of nature, but dismissed the idea as nonsensical. Now, these scientists were reciting long-standing theoretical and experimental evidence of their even tinier component parts.

The psychiatrist found himself intrigued by the application of concepts such as quantum uncertainty, wave-particle duality, and quantum entanglement to human behavior and psychiatry.

Most of what was said bounced off the CIA man like protons colliding in a particle accelerator, his mind fixated instead on the presence of a major project at Area 51 of which he was unaware. His questions about its location were deflected. He learned only that it was underground; somewhere far below their already subterranean location.

"It all comes down to this, gentlemen," the elder scientist said. "For our experiment to effect the teleportation of Mister Robinson, we will utilize the electromagnetic fields generated within the accelerator to propel electron beams to an energy level sufficient to create conditions under which a fleeting black hole will emerge, which will form the mouth of a wormhole that will transport our cowboy back to whence he came."

The younger physicist erased (for the umpteenth time) the chalkboard. His superior stood, buttoned his lab coat, and said, "Gentlemen, let's be on our way."

The CIA man perked up. "To the accelerator?"

With a smile, the physicist said, "Afraid not. That is but where our experiment begins. Rather, we'll be going up to the surface, to where our experiment ends."

A shudder passed through Rawhide Robinson. Hearing his uncertain future referred to as an "experiment" unsettled the cowboy. Even a lifelong penchant for pursuing adventure, exploring possibility, and grabbing for the brass ring at every opportunity could not prepare one for the eventuality facing him today.

As the elevator whisked the party upward, the senior physicist inquired about the group's familiarity with the function of a Faraday cage. The phrase "Never heard of it" sums up the response. And so he held forth briefly on the function of said device. Simply put, he said, a Faraday cage creates a protective shell around something or someone you wish to shield from electrostatic charges or electromagnetic radiation by distributing the charge or radiation around the cage's exterior.

"We have taken the basic concept of the Faraday cage and reversed it," the physicist said. "Rather than keeping the charge out, we have reversed polarity, so to speak. Our cage focuses the energy inward, even intensifies it. Since my young colleague here made the calculations and worked out the equations involved, he will expand on my explanation at the site."

Like subatomic particles focused by an accelerator, the men walked single file out of the elevator, out of the big tin building, and across a dusty patch of asphalt to one of the similar, if smaller, buildings in the complex. To the cowboy, the buildings still looked like giant tomato cans split down the middle and plopped on the desert floor.

As his eyes adjusted from the exterior glare to the dim interior, Rawhide Robinson saw a big ball, about twice as tall as he was, fashioned from metal rods arranged in geometric patterns. Overflowing with enthusiasm and flooded with exuberance, the young physicist gushed forth his story about the device while his superior picked up a wall phone to speak with someone deep down in the very bowels of the earth upon which they stood.

"What you are seeing here," the junior scientist said, "is a geodesic polyhedron sphere of conductive material. The energy beam generated by the accelerator enters its grid via attenuation from outgoing transmissions, with attenuation varied by waveform and frequency. The applied electromagnetic fields will produce forces on the charge carriers—in this case, electrons—within the conductor for redistribution."

The young man in the white lab coat hopped around like spit on a sheet iron stove, pointing out this and that, caressing components, admiring the apparatus, and patting and petting parts and pieces of his invention.

"High flux and pulsed time structures should change the relativistic speed, create both linear and circular polarization, and result in synchrotron radiation, triggering electrostatic discharges and, finally, an electromagnetic pulse. The cage is designed to release the pulse as a non-point-source surge, or burst, of electromagnetic energy. Within the energy field, our calculations suggest a transitory, or fleeting, black hole may form and a wormhole develop."

The smiling physicist turned to the cowboy. "At which point you, Rawhide Robinson, should be absorbed into the hole to be ejected as precisely as our equations allow at or near the time and place of the lightning strike to which we owe your presence among us." The white-coated scientist clapped his hands and clasped them together, shaking with excitement. "I can hardly wait!"

Rawhide Robinson watched the smiling man for a moment, then said. "Tell me something, young feller—how tight is your dally on this deal?"

The physicist looked as blank at the cowboy's question as Rawhide Robinson thought he must have looked while the scientist held forth with his lingo. "What I mean is, in amongst all your highfalutin palaver I swear I heard the words 'suggest' and 'should' and 'may' and such like. Just how sure is this bet?"

By now the senior physicist was back among them. "I can answer that," he said. "Mister Robinson, all I can offer is our confidence in our calculations and the science. At the same time, I am compelled to inform you that the science in this case is entirely theoretical—there are no experiments relevant to our hypothesis nor has there been practical testing of our apparatus."

The assembled party sensed a hum, a vibration, radiating from the floor, growing ever stronger. "Ah, the accelerator is in operation," the elder scientist said. "At least we know that component of our experiment is functioning as anticipated."

Rawhide Robinson walked around the cage, trying to find some sense of security. As the vibration in the floor started to pulse, he noticed the metal seat in the cage, looking altogether like a child's swing hanging in an apple tree, start swaying gently on its chains.

The CIA man stared at the floor, as if he could somehow see through the concrete and the intervening dirt and rocks to identify the source of the throbbing energy, still stunned that such a sizable project existed beneath his very nose, so to speak, yet beyond his knowledge. The psychiatrist studied the demeanor of the physicists, seeking a chink in their armor, a hint of indecision, an intimation of impending danger.

The psychiatrist looked at the CIA man.

The CIA man looked at the psychiatrist.

They each shrugged, accepting a situation that, if uncertain, seemed as logical as any alternative. It was, they thought, entirely up to the cowboy.

All eyes turned to Rawhide Robinson.

"What the heck. I ain't never shied away from adventure in all my born days," he said with a wide smile.

He cinched his thirteen-gallon hat down tight. "Let's do this thing. I suppose the worst that could happen is I'll light up like that big neon cowboy waving howdy at folks down in Las Vegas."

Chapter Forty

Eric Harris watched the dust settle on the gravel road after Rawhide Robinson rode away in the government sedan. Firing up the motorbike, he raised his own dust as he hurried back to Alamo. He not only braved the paved streets of the town where sometimes under-age drivers were called to account by the law, he sought out Alamo police chief Lamar Argyle. He found the police cruiser parked at the Wagon Wheel café and the lawman inside sipping coffee and forking up wedges of a doughnut.

“Sit down,” Argyle said. “What are you up to, Eric?”

“Rawhide’s gone.”

“Gone? Gone where?”

“He wanted to go out there where he says the 51 Ranch used to be, y’know. So I took him.”

“Hungry?” Argyle asked the boy.

“Nah. I’d have a root beer, though.”

The lawman laughed. “Just like ol’ Rawhide, eh?”

Eric smiled. “I guess.”

After Eric stained his upper lip with root beer foam, Argyle asked about the cowboy.

“He was just lookin’ around saying, ‘this was here, that was there’ and stuff like that, y’know. Then this car came by on the road. Went past, then stopped and backed up. Three guys got out and one of them talked to Rawhide for a while.”

“You hear what they talked about?”

“Yeah, sure. He said they wanted to ask him—Rawhide—some questions. Rawhide, I don’t think he wanted to go at first, y’know, on account of he said that guy threatened to shoot him before. But then that guy said if he would come, they could maybe send Rawhide back where he came from. After he said that, Rawhide said he’d go.”

Argyle’s fork stopped halfway to his mouth. “Send him back? He said that?”

“Well, kinda, y’know. Something about some scientists or something.” Eric drained the root beer from his glass. “I tried to tell him not to go, Mister Argyle. I tried to tell him! But he went anyway. Who knows what they’ll do to him out there?”

“I wouldn’t worry about that, son. I don’t know what all they get up to out at that site, but I doubt Rawhide will come to any harm—especially since they know you know he’s out there.”

“What can we do?”

"Not much we can do, Eric. From what you say, Rawhide went of his own free will. Could be they'll turn him loose again, like they did last time."

"No! We've got to do something!"

"Eric, you'd best be getting home."

The boy stopped in the doorway and said, "By the way, mister Argyle. Rawhide, he said to thank you for all you did for him."

At home, Eric opened the refrigerator and made himself a peanut butter and jelly sandwich, carried it into the living room and turned on the television. It all served to remind him of Rawhide Robinson, and the cowboy's fascination with everyday things.

As he munched the sandwich, he noticed Rawhide Robinson's neatly folded chaps on the floor at the end of the sofa, the cowboy's spurs nesting atop them. *He might need those!*

Eric stuffed what was left of the sandwich into his mouth and swept up the chaps and spurs on his way out the door. He hung the spurs on the motorbike's handlebars and laid the chaps over the seat and sat on them, stomped on the kick starter and headed for the desert. *Maybe they've already let him go. Maybe I'll find him on the road again.*

The engine whined at full throttle as Eric passed the old 51 ranch and, later, the place he'd almost ran into the cowboy. He continued on, his passage marked by a rooster tail of dust that lingered for a time then drifted down through the still air to rejoin the desert. A locked gate, plastered with a plethora of "warning" and "no trespassing" and "danger" and "restricted area" and other such signs marked the boundary of Area 51. The boy rolled to a stop, turned the key, and listened to the ticking of the cooling engine.

Eric heaved the motorcycle onto its kickstand and laced his fingers through the chain link gate, looking for any sign of the cowboy. The road showed little evidence of traffic, but the few tread marks in the dust and gravel looked recent. The view through the gate showed no sign of human activity, and, beyond the existence of the road, no indication of human presence. Only the desert—sagebrush, greasewood, shadscale, yucca, bunchgrass, rabbit brush, tumbleweeds, Joshua trees, and the few other scrubby plants able to survive the aridity.

But somewhere out there, Eric knew, there were people. And one of them was Rawhide Robinson.

As he stared across the dun-colored hills and swales and mountains and valleys marching off into the distance, he sensed, as much as saw, a bright flash miles away beyond a line of rough knolls. Eric wondered if the government was testing atomic bombs as they had in years past. But the flash was not as bright, nor was it followed by the wind and thunder and mushroom cloud that accompanied nuclear blasts.

He wondered if Rawhide Robinson saw the flash, and what the cowboy might think of such a thing. After watching and waiting until the sun hung low in the western sky, Eric heaved a big sigh, wiped the muddy grit from around his eyes and off his cheeks and pointed the little motorcycle back toward Alamo.

Although he already suspected as much, it dawned on Eric then and there that he had seen the last of Rawhide Robinson.

Chapter Forty-One

Like a bird on a perch, Rawhide Robinson sat on the metal plank seat of the swing, hands grasping the chains upon which it dangled from the top of the cage. The cage was made entirely of metal—or, as the young physicist who designed and built it would say, "conductive material." The cowboy marveled at the way the rods and bars intersected in straight lines and angles to create a big, round, ball—or, again in the words of the junior scientist, "a geodesic polyhedron sphere." He sensed a slight tingling in the palms of his hands, intensifying in time with the pulsing hum radiating up through the concrete floor.

Across the room, the physicists stood at a control panel behind a leaded glass screen, reading meters, flipping switches, and adjusting knobs. Beyond them, the CIA man in the rumpled suit leaned against the wall, firing up a cigarette with his silver Zippo lighter. The psychiatrist stood outside the cage, staring intently at the cowboy on his swing. He untied the knot in his bowtie, allowing the ends to dangle, and unbuttoned his collar.

"Rawhide," he said.

The cowboy looked at the doctor. "Yes?"

“Are you sure you want to do this?”

Rawhide Robinson scratched his chin whiskers and it dawned on him he was past due for a shave. “Well, Doc, I don’t believe ‘sure’ is the word I’d use.”

“We can stop this right now, you know.”

“Oh, no! I am sure I don’t want to do that.”

“You’re not afraid?”

The cowboy laughed. “The way I see it, Doc, a man’d have to be plumb loco not to be afraid at a time like this.”

“Then why go on?”

“I guess it’s part of bein’ a cowboy. Doing dumb things that might be dangerous is all part of the job. Buckin’ horses, ornery cows, stampeding herds, tangled ropes—cowboyin’ can be one wreck after another. You learn soon enough to grit your teeth, take ahold with your spurs, and give a bronc his head. You could end up planted like a daisy—but you might ride out the storm and be a better cowboy for it. The thing is, if you don’t ante up, you won’t never win the pot.”

The doctor mulled over the cowboy’s philosophical sojourn for a time. Then, “What’s the ‘pot’ you’re hoping to win here?”

“Just wantin’ to get back home, Doc. Leastways to what passes for home to a footloose cowboy.”

“Do you dislike it so much here?”

"Can't say I dislike it, as such. I suppose if I was to find a ridin' job somewheres I'd get used to this here world. But there's just too much that's different—too many people, for one thing. And some of the folks I've met.... Well, I'll just say the herd could stand to be culled some."

Rawhide Robinson lifted his thirteen-gallon lid and raked his fingers through his hair and reset the hat, then grabbed the chains to steady himself in the swing. "That, and, well, things move too fast. Riding a freight train haulin' cattle is all the faster I ever been before now, and that's plenty fast. These automobiles—and, heaven forbid, them aeroplanes—can upset a man's equilibrium. Give me a good horse on a high lope anytime. That covers plenty enough country for this cowboy."

The psychiatrist watched Rawhide Robinson for a time but with all his education, all his diplomas, all his certifications, all his credentials, he could find no fault in the cowboy's logic. He wondered, if facing a similar situation, if he would find the quiet courage that, to Rawhide Robinson, was nothing more than normal—simply put, The Cowboy Way.

The humming and thrumming of the particle accelerator far below had grown in intensity until the entire building resonated.

“Rawhide!” one of the physicists shouted from behind the barrier. “Are you ready?”

The cowboy squirmed into a deeper seat in the swing and adjusted his grip on the chains. “I reckon so.”

“Doctor! You’d better come over here, behind the screen,” the senior scientist said. “You, too,” he said to the CIA man.

“Ten!” the young physicist said as he flipped a switch.

He twisted a knob. “Nine!”

“Eight!” as he plugged a cable into a jack.

He pushed a button. “Seven!”

“Six!” he said, pulling a plug.

With the crank of a dial, “Five!”

“Four!” and he adjusted a lever.

The scientist toggled a toggle. “Three!”

“Two!” he said, as he turned a knob.

Perspiration beaded the physicist’s forehead as he grasped the big, bright red handle of the double-pole switch on the control panel.

The CIA man exhaled a cloud of smoke and clicked his ballpoint pen.

The senior physicist donned goggles with smoked-glass lenses.

The psychiatrist held a deep breath and grasped the edge of the counter.

Rawhide Robinson smiled.

"One!"

The burst of electromagnetic energy blew the big sliding doors right off the end of the Quonset building. Had there been any windows, they, too, would have been sacrificed in the name of experimental physics.

All four witnesses picked themselves up off the floor and dusted themselves off. Only the senior physicist could see clearly, and then only after he realized his dim sight resulted from the goggles he wore. The other men blinked and squinted and rubbed at their eyes with clenched fists.

Wisps of smoke drifted from the seams and slots in the control panel. Sparks and arcs flashed and flared and snapped and sizzled from time to time. Residual electricity sparkled and skittered around the cage like the blue sparks that danced on the tips of the horns of stampeding steers.

Inside, the swing swayed slowly to and fro.

"He's gone," the young physicist said.

"Did it work?" the CIA man said, brushing the lapels of his rumpled jacket.

"It appears so," the senior scientist said. "Rawhide Robinson has most assuredly been teleported from this place."

“Either that, or you vaporized him,” the psychiatrist said.

Chapter Forty-Two

Rawhide Robinson's eyes involuntarily squinted tight in the bright light. Ever so slowly, he peeled one eyelid ever so slightly open. Then the other. Then he raised his eyelids to half-mast and waited until his optical apparatus grew accustomed to the harsh light. The world within his field of vision was fuzzy and unfocused, a faint web of dim shadows the only deviation in the glare.

As awareness returned, the cowboy grew mindful of aches and pains in every nook and cranny of his carcass. His head, in particular, was painful, throbbing with every beat of his heart. He imagined he had been trampled by a herd of stampeding steers, and his head was now crushed in an anvil as a brawny blacksmith pounded it back into shape with repeated and rhythmic blows of his heavy hammer.

Hoping to take his mind off his painfully pulsing brain, he took inventory of his frame and tested its ability to function. He flexed his toes inside his boots. Rotated his ankles. Bent his knees. Twisted his hips. Arched the articulations in his back. Expanded his rib cage. Hunched his shoulders. Jacked his jaws. Wiggled his ears. Flapped—albeit gently—his arms. Crooked his elbows. Tilted his wrists. Stretched his fingers. The activity convinced the uncomfortable cowboy he was, indeed, still among the living. Given his current condition, feeling as he did, he was not sure that fact pleased him.

Blinking repeatedly, he brought the web of shadows above into focus. Branches, limbs, and twigs they were, scorched bare and burned black. The remains of a tree, he decided. While he seemed to be dry, the ground beneath Rawhide Robinson felt damp. He turned his head to one side and saw a saddled horse—his horse, he realized—a few rods away, nosing out mouthfuls of grass on the hillside. Turning the other way, he could see the valley below. There appeared to be nothing there but the usual desert scrub, albeit with jewels of remnant raindrops glistening in the sunlight.

Slowly, gingerly, gently, he raised himself on his elbows, then, with the palms of his hands, pushed his upper half upright. He rested for a time, seated under the charred tree. Carefully removing his thirteen-gallon hat, he attempted to scratch his head until pain convinced him otherwise, replaced the hat, then rubbed his face vigorously.

As much as his body felt discombobulated, the cowboy found his mind even more disjointed, disorganized, and dislocated. He scanned the landscape and eventually realized where he was and why he was there—sort of. A vague, teasing memory told him he was somewhere upslope on the Papoose Range, above Emigrant Valley and the dry playa of Groom Lake. It came to him that he is a cowboy.

With that realization, it all rushed back. He is in Nevada, working on a ranch…the 51 Ranch…the owner is a man named Dominique Elizondo…the cow boss is Matthew Brooks…Matt sent him out here to check on cattle, spread from hell to breakfast in this dry country…then again, not so dry—he got caught in a rainstorm; a duck drowning, frog-strangling, gully-washer…he took shelter under a cedar tree…there was thunder and lightning all around…that's it! Lightning must have struck the tree….

The sky is clear blue and the sun bright now. But the damp soil, occasional drip-drops from blackened branches, and puddles reflecting sunlight from the bed of Groom Lake below verify his memory of the storm.

And the lightning bolt must be the reason for his addled brain and aching body.

As the neurons realigned in his brain, other images poked and prodded their way into memory. Strange, unusual, fantastic recollections—flashes of adventures so bizarre, so outlandish they could only be dreams; impressions conjured up by an unconscious mind.

Buggies and wagons and bicycles that propel themselves at unfathomable speeds. Strange foods in unfamiliar places. Flashing, dancing, colored lights brighter than fire. Giant machines, bigger and noisier than the engine on a freight train, that fly through the sky like gliding birds. Small rooms that rise and fall, letting you out at a different place than where you got in. Girls dancing in a public show wearing nothing but feathers. Cowboys heading and heeling steers in a pen in the middle of a city. A city where thousands of people come to frequent commodious gambling parlors.

And on and on and on—fantastic, phantasmagoric, fanciful, farfetched impressions stirred and roiled and rushed and whirled and perturbed his befuddled and bewildered brain.

It occurred to Rawhide Robinson, the renowned raconteur, that these hallucinatory happenings would make fine fodder for campfire and bunkhouse tales.

But, no, these mirages of memory were too outlandish, too outrageous, too preposterous for public presentation.

No, no one would even listen to, let alone believe, such wild and whimsical yarns.

He himself could make no sense of it. As real as the flashbacks and glimpses and insights seemed, at the same time they seemed too bizarre to be believed.

Rawhide Robinson could not comprehend how such nonsensical foolishness—such hooey and hogwash, such balderdash and baloney, such folly and fatuity—could ever happen. Not in real life. Not in a vivid imagination. Not in whimsy or flights of fancy. No, such nonsense could not even be conjured up in a dream.

Best to just dismiss it. Set it aside. Erase it from memory. Forget it ever happened.

The cowboy wagged his head vigorously in an attempt to shake the illusory images out of his muddled mind like a soggy dog shedding excess water after a swim. He made his way gingerly to his feet and extended his arms in a wide stretch, flexing and wiggling his creaky carcass.

His pants fell down around his knees.

Too shocked and surprised to even attempt to cover himself in an automatic and impulsive attempt to avoid embarrassment, he merely looked down at the bunched britches in wonder. As he hoisted his trousers, it occurred to him for the first time that his chaps were missing. Further investigation revealed metal buttons missing from the fly of his jeans. All that was left were withered and wasted buds. Lacking no reasonable explanation, he imagined the lightning bolt must have melted the fasteners.

Looking further down, he also saw his spurs were unaccountably missing from their accustomed place on the heels of his boots.

Confused and confounded, Rawhide Robinson reached down and hiked up his britches. With no buttons to prevent future falling, no chaps to hug them to his hips, he reached into a vest pocket in search of a length of whang leather to secure the pants in their proper and functional upright position.

He poked and prodded, fished and fiddled among the detritus in the pocket, seeking the feel of a leather string. He fished out some poker chips with "Betty's Coyote Springs Ranch" written on them. Somewhere among the contents, he felt an unfamiliar shape, another unexpected occupant of the pocket and pulled it out for ocular examination.

It was a cylinder, some six inches long, similar in circumference to his pinky finger. A stubby stub stuck out one end and he pressed it with his thumb.

Click.

The familiar sound triggered a whole new panoply of mental pictures. A man with a bowtie asking curious questions and writing down the answers. A high-ranking military officer. Soiled doves listening to his stories. Men in white coats furiously scratching line after line and row upon row of figures and symbols. And a gruff man in a rumpled city suit who smoked like a locomotive and incessantly clicked and clicked and clicked at a curious writing instrument identical to one he held his hand.

Could it all be real?

Could it have happened?

Could these be memories, rather than dreams?

Rawhide Robinson's mind writhed and recoiled at the thought. It couldn't be.

Or could it?

The confounded cowboy, the befuddled buckaroo, the rattled ranahan, the overwhelmed waddy found himself sinking deeper and deeper into a quicksand of sixes and sevens.

So he decided to do the one thing he knew best: ride.

As the sun slipped slowly behind the summit of the Papoose Range, Rawhide Robinson followed his long shadow across the empty expanse of the alkali flat called Groom Lake in the direction of 51 Ranch headquarters and, mayhap, one day, the range beyond; ever riding toward the possibility—the hope—the desire—the wish—the dream—of further adventures of bravery and daring in the Wild West.

About the Author

Winner of four Western Writers of America Spur Awards and a Spur Award finalist on six other occasions, and recipient of two Western Fictioneers Peacemaker Awards and a four-time finalist, Rod Miller writes fiction, poetry, and history about the American West. A lifelong Westerner raised in a cowboy family, Miller is a former rodeo contestant, worked in radio and television production, and is a retired advertising agency copywriter and creative director. Miller's award-winning poetry and short stories have appeared in numerous anthologies, and several magazines have carried his byline.

Find the author online at:

writerRodMiller.com
writerRodMiller.blogspot.com, and
RawhideRobinson.com

Upcoming New Release

SILVER SCREEN COWBOY

BY

ROD MILLER

Latigo Brown is a cowboy. A *real* cowboy, not like those TV and movie cowboys who ride everywhere at a high lope firing off six-shooters and hardly ever come into contact with a cow. But he finds himself lured to Hollywood by a rodeo hero, where he unexpectedly becomes a box-office star. Amidst the glitter and glamour of the movie business, he still harbors resentment for the way he—and other cowboys—are portrayed.

Will Latigo Brown swallow his pride and pocket the money? Will the starlets, the luxuries, the acclaim, the big bucks turn his head? Or will the lure of the ranch and rodeo arena and real cowboys overcome all that? Ride along with Latigo Brown and find the answers in the pages of *Silver Screen Cowboy*.

SPUR AWARD-WINNING AUTHOR
ROD MILLER

For more information
visit: www.SpeakingVolumes.us

GREG HUNT

WESTERNS

www.ingramcontent.com/pod-product-compliance
Lightning Source LLC
Chambersburg PA
CBHW030932260626
47169CB00002B/445

* 9 7 8 1 6 4 5 4 0 6 9 5 2 *